Belar has made lyin

know him as a mild mannered music teacher, but to his fellow monster hunters he's a senior agent with one of the best track records in the organization. Werewolves, malignant spirits, and other oddities—you name it, he can track it. And kill it if necessary.

But when a vampire shows up in Belar's parlor, his two worlds crash into each other. The vampire is named Cassian, and if he had any sense of decency he would be dead since Belar has already tried to kill him. Twice. Luckily, Cassian isn't interested in holding a grudge. He wants to hire the hunter. Someone in vampire society wants Cassian dead and they've been using Belar to do their dirty work. Finding the culprit will save them both.

Their search for answers takes them through a nighttime world of ancient vampires, demon tailors, and monsters of pure shadow. But Belar hasn't been the only one lying, and enemies and allies are harder to tell apart in the dark.

From the Dark We Came

Pointy Ears and Pointy Teeth, Book One

J. Emery

A NineStar Press Publication

Published by NineStar Press
P.O. Box 91792,
Albuquerque, New Mexico, 87199 USA.
www.ninestarpress.com

From the Dark We Came

This is a work of fiction. Names, characters, places, and incidents are either the product of the author's imagination or are used fictitiously. Any resemblance to actual persons living or dead, business establishments, events, or locales is entirely coincidental.

Printed in the USA
First Edition
March, 2020

Print ISBN: 978-1-951880-71-2

Also available in eBook, ISBN: 978-1-951880-70-5

Warning: This book contains sexually explicit content, which may only be suitable for mature readers, fantasy typical violence and injury, minor character death, beheading, blood, blood drinking, and blood magic.

To all my fellow arthritic monster hunters

Chapter One

Vibrant pink and amber dawn streaked the sky before Belar finally clambered down from his perch in a nearby tree. He moved with spidery grace. Heights had never bothered him, not when he had perfected the art of sneaking out of his bedroom window before the age of six. He had only gotten better since then. Nothing soothed like a narrow ledge beneath his fingers and a world of sky behind him, waiting to catch him if he fell. Granted, the fall would most likely kill him. But until then—pure ease.

He should have been born a bird instead of a man.

The abandoned house was silent. He had searched the area for days before he'd found the place, half swallowed by the encroaching forest. The perfect place for a vampire to hide, empty as it was, but not so distant from human society to make feeding difficult.

There had been a brief moment earlier when he had even worried his guess was wrong, and the house really was as empty as it appeared despite the feel in the air—blood possibly—that called to him. Then he'd gotten his first sighting as the vampire had come lurching back to his nest and removed any lingering doubt. Belar had gauged him as average height (for a vampire as they ran tall) and probably quite old based on the speed of his movements. He wasn't graceful—exhaustion rendered him clumsy—but he was certainly fast. Belar had lost track of him for seconds at a time as the vampire zigzagged through the dense underbrush in the woods. But by now the vampire should be fast asleep, hidden away where the sun couldn't disturb him or his rest.

Belar had waited an extra hour to be certain. Not that he was worried. Because he wasn't.

Vines grew thick over the sides of the old house, its sagging roof full of patched holes, half the windows empty staring eyes, their glass long since shattered. Utterly abandoned. Dilapidated. Save for the curtains hanging in a lower room, a cheerful, if faded pattern of blue on white like the border on a fancy plate. They had no reason to be there. Not here in an empty house, in an empty town where all but the birds had moved on. Even the bones of those caught in the fire that had destroyed the village years ago were gone. The forest had reclaimed everything but a handful of houses, their crumbling walls marked by smudges of soot and a few scattered patches of paving stone that had once been the town square. The bridge arching over the nearby stream verged on collapse. The rest was mossy, green, and still.

His eyes strayed again to the curtains in the window. Something about them unsettled him.

"Or maybe you're just losing your touch after the last time," he muttered. In the stillness, his voice sounded loud as a shout, and he flinched despite himself. But anyone was liable to be a bit jumpy after his recent near miss, he reasoned.

His last hunt had begun as they typically did. Weeks of research and information gathering about the area before he successfully pinpointed the resting place of the vampire and felt safe making his move. He'd always been thorough. Usually it served him well. But despite his many precautions, despite waiting for the sun to rise high enough to assure his target was deeply asleep, Belar had found himself trapped in a tomb with a very angry and very *awake* vampire who was fully capable of fighting back. Belar had recovered from the blow that threw him into the wall just in time to see the dark figure of the vampire eclipsing the sun streaming in the open door. For one moment, as impossibly beautiful as a wrathful god to Belar's dazed mind. Then he ran out into the daylight. Everyone knew what happened to vampires touched by the sun. No part was pleasant. No one seemed to have told this vampire though. There were no screams. No flames. Not even the slightest sizzle of searing flesh. Nothing but a rapidly retreating vampire.

Belar had been lucky to escape with nothing worse than a black eye, a sprained wrist, and enough cracked ribs to make breathing exciting for the next few weeks. In a lifetime of brushes with death, this had been the closest of all. By rights he really should be dead. Not that he was complaining on the last point.

And clearly he hadn't learned his lesson well enough since here he was stalking yet another vampire. Other hunters might have taken the job if he'd wanted to give it up. The thought had never even occurred to him.

Belar slithered in through one of the gaping eyehole windows and landed softly atop a floor carpeted with moldy leaves and splintered wood that had once been a shutter. He took a moment to get his bearings. There wasn't much to see. He'd surveyed the house from every imaginable angle outside, but hadn't ventured inside. He hadn't dared. The risk of spreading his scent around and alerting the vampire to his presence was too great. Now it wouldn't matter. The sun was up and so was the vampire's time.

The stairs leading to the cellar were almost completely broken away. What remained was as rotten as everything else in this place. A few jagged timbers and a yawning darkness below. He would have to be careful climbing back up so he didn't end up full of splinters.

Belar checked his axe and the knives strapped to his wrists before he snugged the knot of the scarf tied over his face. Then he leaped down to kill himself a vampire.

*

"Did everything go well this time?" Merriville asked as Belar trudged into headquarters. The director of the hunters' organization had the starchy posture of someone who spent a great deal of time in suits and the vague stare of someone who needed to clean his glasses more often. If he'd ever been a field agent, it must have been a long time ago. Belar had known him to get lost just walking through the archives. Merriville's lip curled up as he caught sight of Belar. "Ah. I assume so." He took an unsubtle step backward to let Belar pass.

Belar nearly snarled at the little man. The only thing keeping him from doing so was the fact Merriville, and his abysmal tweed suit, was nominally in charge of making sure Belar got his government sanctioned hunter's fee every month.

He knew he looked terrible, and possibly smelled terrible, but he felt even worse. Maybe it was the vampire blood he had swallowed. The scarf he wore over the lower half of his face when he hunted had slipped just as he'd beheaded the vampire and black blood had gotten everywhere: in his mouth, on his glasses, even into his ear. Down his shirt. There was a persistent itch where it had dried to a crust on his chest. He needed a bath.

But in all other respects, the hunt had been a success. The vampire hadn't stirred until Belar's axe cleaved head from neck, and then he had simply withered away, leaving nothing but a curl of shadow and the spray of viscous black blood that had painted

Belar from nose to knee. It was textbook. One fewer vampire menacing the countryside all thanks to him and his efforts. Good job, team.

He *should* be pleased.

He wasn't.

In fact he was nearly the exact opposite of pleased. Two steps to the left and he would be there. Displeased.

It was those fucking blue curtains in the window. And the neat little stack of books he had later found in the room with that window, a partially burnt stump of candle beside them.

What kind of vampire set about murdering his way through the countryside and then returned to his nest to read pastoral poetry?

"Are you absolutely *sure*—" he began, whirling back to face Merriville only to find him gone. Probably disappeared back to his office. Belar hadn't even heard him scuttle away. Damn him.

The room was silent and peaceful. The stained-glass windows running along one wall fractured the light into greens and golds and blues, and at midmorning like this, he was unlikely to run into anyone else who was working. Belar took his time filing his report, typing everything out on the typewriter with careful pecks so that he wouldn't make too many mistakes and have to begin again. His hands at least were clean. His gloves had taken the worst of it, being closest to the business end of the axe, and those he could remove. There wasn't even a single flake of black blood beneath his nails. The rest of him probably looked like a nightmare, and he didn't relish the idea of trying to wash out the blood clotted in his long black hair, but his hands were clean.

Belar glared at the little boxes on the report as he aligned the typewriter to fill the empty spaces.

Location. Description. Date. Current status. That last one was easy. It was always the same: *deceased/closed.* He had an entire drawer of filed reports, all of them marked just the same way. All except for the hunt before this anyway.

He reread the preliminary information again as he turned the platen and hit the carriage return to begin adding his final notes.

Vampires were known to be fierce and agile predators. Ruthless. Only a few centuries ago they had rampaged unchecked, killing more people in a single night of bloodlust than most plagues did in a year. Now they'd been driven back to the shadows they originated from and Belar, or other hunters like him, dealt with any real and sustained threat to the human population. After all, it was their world, and they should get to live in it. Or so went the general reasoning. It was a dangerous but necessary job, and the pay was commensurate with that risk.

Today's vampire was suspected of having spirited away no fewer than ten people from a nearby village in the last few months before word was relayed back to headquarters, and Belar was assigned. Ten gone. There'd been no sign of any of them at the crumbling little house, but perhaps the vampire had been clever and buried them in the woods. Or thrown them into a river. There were any number of ways to dispose of bodies. Belar knew plenty himself. Not every hunt was as easy to cover as vampires. There had been plenty of cases where he'd spent nearly as long collecting leftover *things* from the site as he had in finding the target. Compared to that, vampires practically cleaned up after themselves. Today's unfortunate mess aside. A strike, a whiff of acrid smoke, and the job was complete so he could return to file his report.

But nearly a dozen people dead and not a single bone or splatter of blood... That had been unexpected.

The typewriter rattled the desk as he worked, filling line after line, and trying not to think of blue curtains and a curious absence of bodies.

*

By the time he had finished his report, filed it, put the duplicate into Merriville's mail slot to be collected, and checked for any new hunts in the queue, it was nearly midday and the silence was giving way to the quiet murmur of voices. There were never more than a few hunters around at any given time. Most lived in or around the city until they rated their own door linking spell and were able to move further out as Belar had. His spell was attached to an unused closet in his house and allowed him to come and go from headquarters almost as he pleased. He had only to open his closet and step straight through into the lobby. No travel necessary. It was also why he tended to pull the more far-flung hunts so the door spell was something of a mixed blessing.

Today there were only two hunters in besides him, heads bent together over a file open on one of the long worktables in the front room. The first belonged to Marta, a hunter who favored hauntings and, near as Belar could tell from the few times they'd worked together, getting thrown into open graves. She was also barely over five feet on a good day, and anytime she needed a book off the high shelves Marta decided to make Belar her own personal valet. The other hunter was Horace, a tall, broad man with a craggy face like a stone wall. Actually, everything about him had always struck Belar as being rather stony, but something had been chipping away at him since his accident in the field earlier this year. Horace bordered on gaunt compared to the last time they'd run into each other. It couldn't have been more than a couple of months, but the difference made it seem longer. He could have been two different people. Horace Before and Horace After.

Belar gave the two a wide berth and hoped not to be spotted. He always felt a little mean while covered in gore. They would understand.

"Ah, you are here. I thought I heard your terrible typing," Marta said, waving him over. Her dark hair was a mound of curls today, and there was a smudge of something greenish on one of her pale-brown cheeks. Very possibly mold. It wouldn't have been the first time. "Come help us."

"I would rather not if it's all the same."

Horace raised his eyes from the file on the table. Open books lay arrayed around them, woodcut illustrations staring out from many of the pages. Bestiaries it looked like. "Don't you look charming." He said it in such a flat way Belar couldn't tell if it was meant merely as a statement or a taunt. It was possibly a little of both. He didn't know Horace particularly well, though Horace had been around longer than most. Longer than Belar, he thought. After fifteen years it was hard to be sure.

Marta made a face. "Oh. You have a little—a lot—of something on you," she said, fishing for her handkerchief and holding it out. She bit her lip. "Vampire again?"

Belar shook his head at the proffered handkerchief. "Yes."

"That's why I stick to ghosts. No mess."

"Except for the occasional bit of entrails," Belar said dryly.

"Oh no, I save those for you." Marta smiled at him, the gap between her front teeth giving it a mischievous look.

"Too kind. Too kind. I'll remember that next time you ask me for help." And since there seemed to be no escape short of turning tail and running, Belar dragged himself over to their table to see what they were so intent on. It made no more sense from close up. “What is all of this?”

“A sudden rash of animal disappearances. Livestock mostly. And a lot of chickens. I want to get it cleared up before it moves on to human prey. Whatever *it* is,” Marta said, pointing at a messily drawn map, obviously her own. He recognized her scribbling. And that really was a *lot* of little *X*s on it. Never a good sign.

Belar’s eyebrows lifted. “You did the usual sweep?”

“Of course. But it was unhelpful at best, so I came back to research the most likely suspects. There must be something here I can use to narrow the search.” Her lower lip turned down in a pout as she blew out an aggravated breath.

“And I’m helping instead of going back home to sleep like a sensible person,” Horace said. He flipped a few pages in one of the books and held it up. “A troll? Do trolls still exist in these parts?”

“You were only loitering and you know it. Your queue has been empty for weeks. If I was you, I would be abusing my recovery leave instead of mooning around this place. Get a hobby or something.” Marta glanced at the description and shook her head. “Doesn’t sound right. And there’s been no confirmed sightings in a century at least. I don’t think I’m that special.”

Belar sighed and perched on the corner of the table. “I could be mistaken, but I don’t think it has anything to do with how special *you* are.”

Marta handed him a book. “It might. You don’t know. Now help me.”

Bascom’s Field Guide of Northern Plants stared up at him. Belar turned it so she could see the spine. “Are you planning to teach it gardening?”

She snatched the book back and threw a different volume into his hands, this one bound in greasy black leather. “I must’ve grabbed the wrong one from the shelf. Try that instead.”

“You know, I had been hoping to sleep sometime this week,” Belar said dismally as he opened the book to the index.

“It’s no use. I said the same thing,” Horace said. He looked Belar over. “How long have you been here? You look foul.”

“Long enough to file my reports and to be entirely too tired for all of this. I have students this afternoon, Marta. I can’t teach them their scales if I smell like I’ve been paddling around in shit. Someone will complain. It may very well be me.” He flipped the book around again to point at a picture of something large and vaguely equine. He didn’t even know what it was or where it was commonly found. Reading the entry was too much for his strained eyes, but it looked promising. “What about this?”

She shook her head. “Already thought of that one.”

He flipped more pages. He couldn't tell if the spots he was seeing were vampire blood on his glasses or a sign of imminent unconsciousness. "Black dog?"

"Now you're just being insulting. Hey, where are you going?" The last was said to Horace as he straightened and headed down the hall toward the offices with surprising speed.

He held up the copy of *Bascom's* but didn't stop. "I thought I would return this for you."

"There's not going to be anything in the queue for you no matter how many times you look, Horace," Marta called.

He turned the corner without answering.

While she was distracted, Belar made his own bid for freedom, hopping off the table and darting toward the main door.

"Wait. Get back here, you traitor. Help me find this thing." She shook a fist but didn't make a move to chase him. Just as well. She would have caught him in seconds if she had.

"Students, Marta. Students who want to give me money, and if I don't get a few hours' sleep soon I'm going to collapse. If you haven't found any leads by tomorrow, send me a note through the fast post, and I'll help you look then," Belar said.

With a wave he tossed the door open and was gone.

Chapter Two

Belar tapped his foot to begin the count, body already swaying into the familiar rhythm of the tune as he lifted his flute to his lips. From the piano beside him came a tentative tinkling of notes. Off tempo. And slightly off-key. A flat when there should have been a natural. He did his best to stay with Millicent no matter how she went astray, but before long she'd left the time signature behind and was forging ahead into the weeds. Still, it wasn't bad for a near beginner student.

Millicent beamed up at him as her little hands slid off the keys and back into her lap. She was one of his newest, and youngest, students. Her feet still didn't reach the floor when she sat on the piano bench, but her long brown hair fell down her back like a curtain, nearly to the seat when she tipped her head to look at him. Her hair was drawn back with a fat blue bow at the nape today to match her creased blue muslin, and her cheeks were two dimpled apples, rosy from the cool weather and from how pleased she was with herself.

Belar felt a moment of fondness so acute it was like he'd been stabbed. He'd never wanted to have children, but sometimes he thought he might not mind borrowing one for a while. Maybe a pair. He just wanted them long enough to dress up splendidly and go for walks in the park. Play a duet (badly—he might be fond of her, but Millicent was still generally atrocious on the piano even after three months of steady practice). All those little domestic details.

He reached out a hand to pat her hair. It was soft but tangled, and his fingers caught in the snarls. He quickly retracted the touch.

Never mind.

He tried smiling benevolently down at her instead. That was safer.

Millicent scooted sideways on the bench to face him, short legs kicking. "I practiced hard," she informed him.

"I can tell," Belar lied. He appreciated her enthusiasm for his lessons if nothing else. "It was very good," he added when she seemed to want more.

She nodded, still beaming, before swinging around to face the keys and raising her hands to attack the unsuspecting ivory. Then she paused and instead picked out a lullaby with one hand, humming along as she searched for the right keys and going back a few times to redo the parts she had gotten wrong. Her face creased in concentration.

And there was that uncomfortable throb of fondness in his heart again.

She was young yet. She could learn the rest in time.

Belar set his flute beside its case atop a nearby table and stretched the kinks from his back as Millicent continued to run through her not-unimpressive library of nursery songs and lullabies. She really was improving. Not quickly, but the effort warmed his heart all the same.

"Is it time for you to go already?" she asked without looking up.

The clock on the mantel showed ten minutes to the hour. "Not quite. But soon, yes. I'd like to hear you try the last song again before I do, and then I'll have a new piece for you to work on until next lesson."

"Mama wanted to invite you to dinner. I wasn't supposed to tell you."

"Oh. Tonight?"

His eyes flicked to the window. It wouldn't be dark for at least another hour, and it wasn't as if he had any other plans for the evening. Sitting with a book maybe. Resting. Now that autumn was growing darker and colder, he was off hunting rotation until spring. Just as well. He'd thought the vampire would be his last hunt of the season, but then the ghost he had been working all year to clear out of a cemetery had sprung up again and ruined his plans. Stubborn incorporeal shit. It had left him a mass of bruises beneath his high-collared shirt and waistcoat, and beneath that was the bone-deep stiffness left behind from overexertion. The chill in the air only exacerbated it. By the time winter set in he would be wrapped in furs like an ancient king in a lonely court, praying before his fireplace for the warmth to unravel him. But that was months away yet. For now he was just stiff and a little creaky.

Sunset was the bigger problem. He hadn't been afraid of the dark since he was a child, but that didn't mean he wanted to be out in it unarmed either. He had good reason to fear. Still, how long could one meal last? And what kind of excuse could he fabricate for leaving that wouldn't risk upsetting his thus far very generous patron? Millicent's mother could be very insistent when she wished to be. Belar didn't know if he had the energy to deflect her or her intended offer of food. Quite good food. He'd only dined with them a few times before, but the memories sat heavy and delicious on his tongue. All that awaited him at home was a bit of cheese and the last fruit from the garden. His hunting wages were late.

Belar fussed with his lace cuffs as he thought. He'd chosen them because he liked the look of the lace but there was no denying how helpful they were for hiding things—like the long scratch across the back of one hand, still a little pink. Fang wounds tended to take forever to heal. This one had been with him for months already.

The full force of Millicent's large, round brown eyes turned on him. Like a puppy. "You will stay, won't you?" It didn't seem possible for her eyes to get bigger and yet they did.

Belar sighed. She was doing it on purpose. He knew she was doing it on purpose. But it was nice to be wanted even if it was only by a small and incredibly manipulative child. "Very well. Just this once."

*

Belar didn't quite walk home. The reality was more of a totter. He had drunk too much and eaten even more, and he was going to pay for all of it. And soon. A hangover might be the least of his troubles given how rubbery his legs felt.

Sometime during dinner the sun had set. It had been in the window, shining pink on his face while Millicent's mother related the latest gossip about all her nearest neighbors and the stories about Mrs. Hastings' missing chicken. Then the next moment the sun had gone, leaving nothing but a darkening sky and unease in its place.

He regretted living on the very edge of town.

The house itself was wonderful, a small cottage with a fruitful garden that kept him in vegetables and healing herbs all summer long. The woods curved along its back, creating an additional wall of privacy. Really it was ideal—certainly better than the last town he had lived in—and the distance from the neighbors made it easier to accommodate a life largely spent crawling around ruins and dark woods, decapitating monsters, without inviting any particularly uncomfortable questions.

For instance, “Where is it you disappear to for a week out of every month?”

Or, “Why do you often come back from these trips limping and covered in blood and ichor?”

Not to mention, “Are your enemies likely to track you here and burn down our houses while trying to get at you?”

The last had yet to come up, but it was difficult to forget the uncomfortably close call when some of his previous neighbors had taken him for a demon and attempted to burn him in his own house. Belar didn’t really blame them. Anyone was bound to be suspicious of a person found hooded and chanting strange incantations during the nighttime hours. They hadn’t known it was a protection spell, and he hadn’t had the chance to explain. Assuming the explanation would have helped at all. More than one unwary witch’s spellwork had ended in slavering jaws full of fangs instead of the magical cure they sought. The newspapers were full of those tales all the time.

After the house fire and midnight flight, Belar had taken pains to always meet his new neighbors, maybe even bring them a bottle of wine or the like. Flowers from his garden when they were in season. He socialized. He patted the heads of small children and pets. And he went out of his way to start a number of conflicting rumors about himself so that no one would think to fabricate exploits for him. At the moment, depending on who you asked, he was a traveling musician, a scholar, or the disinherited child of a wealthy and distant fictional family whose name the listener had almost definitely heard before. The last was his favorite. It was just implausible yet fabulous enough that no one would admit to believing it even as they spread the tale like wildfire.

It was effective. Like leading several different lives at once. And no one guessed he was anything other than what he claimed to be.

Eventually, the time would come when he needed to move on again, as it always did, but until then he was free to enjoy being Belar the musician and tutor (and possible lost heir). He had a bevy of young students about the town and surrounding areas. Not enough to live on but enough to make it seem like he could. And he *did* like the children. They were small, and they asked unusual questions, and he could lie about anything he liked as long as he didn't do it too often. He'd told his youngest student, Foster, that he was the lost son of a dragon after the boy noticed the pointed tips of Belar's ears—which hadn't been his fault. It was hard to maintain a good glamour around children. They saw through to the layer of truth beneath and weren't yet jaded enough to ignore it like they should. Foster had been so dazzled by Belar's story he'd spent an extra hour every day for a month practicing his scales in an effort to hear more.

And it was only a partial untruth. Belar's father was Fae (allegedly), and Belar never *had* met the man. All he had to remember him by were his mother's stories, ears a bit too pointed to be human, and hair the color of sea fog. The ability to glamour away the latter two traits was the only useful gift his absent father had left before disappearing back to the Fae lands or wherever it was errant fathers went. His mother had never said, and Belar had quit asking around the time he stopped going about in pigtails.

There was no way to contact the Fae—not just his father but *any* of them—if they didn't wish to be contacted. They appeared when they wanted, *disappeared* when they wanted, and Belar decided he was better off without them anyway. You couldn't miss what you had never known.

His version of his past was entertaining enough. Lost heirs sounded terribly romantic, and Foster, the darling boy, still looked at Belar as if he was made of stardust.

Of his students, Millicent was least gullible of all, but Belar liked that about her too. She would be a terrifying force someday when she learned how to lie properly. Too bad he would be long gone by then.

Belar stumbled toward his house, pausing every so often to listen. Even with his glasses, the dark was like a curtain, the moon barely enough to keep him from wandering off the road. The night air moved around him. He shivered as it played over his bare neck, lifting tendrils from his ponytail. Then he kept on walking. The longer he lingered in the dark, the more tension flared in him, tightening his muscles as he prepared for attacks that never came.

He was hopelessly drunk. People tended to get the wrong idea about him since he spent so many nights (in the summer when the dark held off for hours) losing at cards in the tavern, but in actuality he drank very little. It was easier to lose if he was sober while he did it. Tonight had been a rare miscalculation. Their house had been so warm and inviting, and for a moment he had felt like he belonged there.

Belar shoved open his door and nearly fell over the threshold.

The dark bothered him less inside. In his own territory. He knew where everything was, so he didn't even need a light to cross the room, stepping around unseen obstacles by muscle memory. He tugged out the ribbon holding his hair back, letting the long dark strands fall about his shoulders, letting Belar the tutor run off him like rain. The tie was next, discarded on a nearby table.

He stretched his shoulders and groaned, twisting until the muscles across his back pulled, the pain spreading all the way down, mixing with the aches in his bones. The pain was better. He'd chosen it. A reminder of the fight. There were rarely ever witnesses—not any who lived anyway. Nothing except for the pain. The bruise over his hip and the long jagged scratch on his shoulders from hitting a tree, those were his keepsakes until they faded. They remembered what he'd done even if no one else would ever know about it. He was going to miss that feeling.

He fell across the sitting room and toward the stairs; tripped his way to his lofted bedroom.

His heart beat like music. Not a slow waltz this time. Something quick. Light. All those sweet little thirty-second notes, like the chirping of birds. It had been a good night for Belar the tutor, a successful recent outing for Belar the hunter. Maybe that was enough.

He saw the shadow out of the corner of his eye, one darkness slipping over another. He was expecting no one.

With one hand he scooped up the glass paperweight from the desk as he turned. It was in midair before he saw the first impression of features of the dark figure emerging from his kitchen. The paperweight shattered where it hit the wall. The figure hadn't seemed to move aside, but they were utterly unharmed. Still moving toward him in the same languid manner. Shadows striped their face. The long hawk-like nose, wide mouth, cheekbones so stark they could draw blood. But it was the amber eyes he found himself staring at as recognition hit him and turned his body to stone. Those eyes seemed to have an unnatural light of their own. They glowed like a cat's.

There was a vampire in his house, and Belar had already failed to kill him once. That morning in the crypt. He could still taste the blood in his mouth as he had watched the vampire disappear into the sunlight. And now he was back.

The vampire advanced. He was tall. They were always so damn tall they made Belar feel small even when he was crouched over them with an axe. It was worse, he realized, to see one standing.

He glanced down to be sure the vampire wasn't floating. They did that sometimes. Maybe it was an intimidation tactic. Maybe they just couldn't help it. Either way, he hated it. But this one stood in a pool of shadow, and he didn't have that telltale bob. The floorboards creaked beneath his feet as he moved closer.

And he still hadn't said a word. If this was a vendetta, Belar wished he would say so. Did this vampire even remember him? They had fought and almost killed each other during the hunt a few months ago. That seemed like it deserved some kind of recognition.

"What do you want?" Belar tried. "How did you get in?"

There should have been protections on the house to avoid this exact situation. He'd spent *hours* on those. Hours and hours of endless chanting. Did this vampire even *know* how tedious that had been? His irritation warred with his good sense; good sense that was telling him he should probably run while he had the chance. But where would he go? The very same privacy he'd moved to the edge of town to preserve also meant there was no chance of ready refuge even if he wanted it. The forest was worse. In the forest, Belar was just another prey animal. A rabbit with longer legs and better hair.

He'd come up against the desk as he backed away, the top mostly scattered with papers, his ledger book for keeping his tutoring fees, another for his hunting expenses. No, that one was put away. Locked in a drawer where no one would find it without hunting for it, which they might do if he wound up dead. His hand closed on the letter opener. Silver, naturally. Everything he owned which could be made of silver was. The tarnish was a nightmare.

The letter opener grazed the vampire's cheek and then stuck in the wall behind him when Belar threw it. He didn't even flinch. Instead, a faint smile painted his lips. The tips of his fangs showed when he did that. "Through the door of course," he said. Amused. "Is there any other way? Your windows are too small. I wouldn't fit. Are you planning to throw more knives at me?" His fingers brushed his cheek. "They sting a bit."

"They're supposed to."

It was like he was asking to be stabbed. Belar could help with that.

His next knife sailed through the dark, aimed at chest height. The vampire wasn't there when it arrived. He'd vanished in a blink. Belar pulled the silver wire he wore on his wrist as a bracelet. He would have rather had an axe. The weight of the weapon did the work for him then. As the vampire lunged from behind him, Belar spun, punching and dodging out of his grasp. His tiny sitting room was hardly fit for fighting. There were too many obstacles. They grappled around the couch and hit the closed front door, Belar aiming quick jabs of his knife between them, but Belar had the distinct impression he was losing. Again.

He grabbed up the nearest candlestick and swung at the vampire's jaw. It connected with a satisfying crack. The vampire grunted and stumbled backward a few steps, momentarily stunned. Belar kicked him in the thigh to unbalance him. Then he pivoted around him, bringing the wire up to loop around the vampire's throat, and pulled it taut.

The vampire made a strangled noise, the air leaving him in a hiss as he clawed at the wire with both hands, but Belar was ready. He yanked in the opposite direction, leaning every bit of his weight into it. The muscles in his back were on fire. His hands were raw from the slide of the wire against his palms. But the wire bit deeper into the vampire's neck, the first drop of blood welling up as he fought Belar.

"Even you can lose your head," Belar growled into the vampire's ear. "All I have to do is tug." Their struggles had pulled them tight together. It was unnerving to feel the slow, slow filling of the vampire's lungs as he took a new breath. There was no sign of fear or strain despite the silver wire wrapped around his throat. "Why did you come here? You could have killed me months ago. Why now?"

The vampire laughed.

And then Belar was tossed across the room. The wire was gone, torn from his hands. He hit the wall hard and slid down, ears ringing, head spinning. His mouth tasted of blood. He tried to rise but a hand closed around his throat, holding him in place. The grip wasn't tight, only enough to drive the point home. A warning. With a vampire's strength it would barely take a thought to separate his head from his shoulders. The vampire bent over him. He was coiled energy like a storm cloud.

"Now that I have your attention," the vampire said, voice a quiet purr. "If I wanted to kill you, you would be dead already. I could have ripped out your throat at least thrice before you walked across the room. You didn't even know I was here."

"So why didn't you?"

The vampire leaned closer and with him came the scent of warmth and spice. "Because I don't want to kill you. I want to hire you."

Belar blinked. Surely, he had heard wrong. His ears were still ringing after his collision with the wall. "What?"

Chapter Three

The vampire sat in Belar's rocking chair, long hands resting lax on the curved arms as though it were a throne and he a king. He certainly had the face for it. Smooth skin the red-brown of cherrywood, hair a cascade of loose dark waves brushing his cheeks. The amber of his eyes obscured by the way they reflected light like mirrors. A crown would suit that brow, those eyes. It was like looking into a lightning storm and knowing you were about to be struck.

He had waited patiently while Belar limped to the couch and fell onto it with a symphony of stifled cries. If Belar was going to die, he might as well do so in comfort.

"Why me?" Belar asked.

"Why not you?"

It was difficult to convey hatred with only a look, but Belar did his best.

The vampire stared back, bemused. Finally, he sighed. "I've been wondering how you found me. My resting place."

"You came all the way here just for that? Was it supposed to be difficult?" Belar sneered.

It had been. He'd spent countless hours following hearsay, bent over books and newspapers searching for any clues. Days more checking every likely bolt-hole. Then checking the unlikely ones. It had begun to feel impossible until he had done it. But this vampire didn't need to know how much time Belar had dedicated to finding him. It felt too much like congratulating him.

"Yes. I made sure of it. Do you have any idea the pains I took to be unfindable? I was supposed to disappear. And yet you found me anyway. I want to know how."

Belar stared at him. "You're hiring me to tell you how I found you?"

"No. I'm hiring you because you hunt vampires, and aside from me, I gather you're quite good at it. Especially the killing part." His smile widened like this was a compliment. Granted, in Belar's line of work it nearly was. He still didn't want to hear it. Not from a vampire. "Hunt someone for me."

"I don't take requests."

The next flash of fangs was intentional. "And I don't recall making any."

Belar's eyes narrowed. "You called it a job. You said you wanted to hire me, but this sounds more like extortion. You haven't even offered to pay me. I don't work for *free*. Or for vampires."

Tension had set deep into his muscles already. Everything hurt. Maybe the pain was making him delirious. Sitting here, talking to a vampire as though it were normal, as though Belar didn't have vampire blood beneath his nails and a knife sticking out of his wall. Only hours ago, he had been contentedly teaching scales, and now his home, *his* sanctuary, had been violated. Rage, hot and acidic, bubbled up in his throat and blotted out anything that might have registered as fear.

The vampire tipped back his head, baring the long column of his throat, humming a low note so close to a growl that Belar shivered. “You want money? Isn’t your life enough?”

“I already have that. It’s not much of a payment. Not when you’ve broken into my home, and I have no reason to trust you or your word.”

The vampire rocked serenely in Belar’s chair, watching him. The only evidence of their earlier fight was the smudged line of blood on his cheek, the cut beneath already healed, a raised red line of irritation where the wire had bitten into his throat, and a tear in the sleeve of his long black coat. He hadn’t had that coat when they fought the first time. Belar wondered where he had gotten it. “Do you?” The vampire reached into an inner pocket of his coat to retrieve something. He tossed it to Belar. “I took care of the first but there’s at least one more on its way here. Work for me and there won’t be.” He smiled again, dropping his chin into his hand as he studied Belar. “Honestly, I thought a hunter would rejoice at the chance to kill more vampires, sanctioned even. This is unexpected.”

Belar opened his hand and almost dropped the thing on the floor when he saw what it was. A canine tooth edged with black decay. Just from the pressure of his grip it had started to crumble. The faint stink of rot clung to it.

"Do you know what that is?" The vampire chuckled as Belar hastily set the tooth on the table and scoured his palm against his trouser leg.

He could still feel the slippery wrongness of the tooth against his skin, as though it had started burrowing into his flesh. He rubbed his hand even harder against his thigh, hoping to blot out the feeling with sheer determination. "Of course, I know a tooth when I see one. And from a shadow beast it looks like. What was it doing in your *pocket*?" *And how could you bear to touch it*, he wanted to ask but didn't.

"Because I took it from the beast after I killed it. Not two miles out of town and headed this direction. You're welcome by the way."

"For?"

"You're not nearly as clever as you think, hunter. *You* were also difficult to find, but someone else has tracked you here, and they want you dead. Unlike me." He smiled again for emphasis. "No one sends only one beast. When they see the first has failed, there will be more. You must have made someone very angry to go to the trouble of sending those beasts."

He'd been thinking much the same thing though he had no clue what he could have done to provoke this kind of attack. Vampires were one thing. Forest beasts. Angry water sprites. The occasional ghost.

He'd gotten rather good at dispatching all of those after so many years. But it was difficult to fight a monster you couldn't even touch. One that wanted nothing but whatever it was told to want. From what he knew, shadow beasts were rare, bordering on mythic, and kept as guard dogs for the most part, enforcers for the more bloodthirsty demons and vampires. He'd never even seen one himself, but he'd heard plenty of stories. All of them seemed to revolve around one piece of advice: if you see one, run. And if you can't run, you're fucked.

Belar stared at his hand. He could still feel the burn of the tooth against his skin. He didn't think he was imagining it.

"All right. Who or what is it you want me to hunt?"

The vampire brightened.

*

Cassian had watched the hunter as he recognized the beast's tooth and immediately blanched. His hand shook as he set it aside. His moods were surprisingly transparent. The vampire liked that about him a little. He had only the vaguest recollection of the hunter from their first encounter, just dark hair and dark eyes and the smell of something...delicious. The last had been a surprise.

Humans always smelled at least a little pleasant, thanks to all that blood coursing through their veins, like multi-course meals on legs, something Cassian had never had to adjust to. He spent so much of his time among his own kind it was a continual shock whenever he ventured beyond to feed and was assailed by the incredible smell of so much humanity. It was a wonder any of the kin could focus on anything else with them around. And he had certainly never encountered a human who smelled quite as good as this one. Or who looked as delicious as he smelled.

Cassian ranged around the hunter's ruined sitting room while the man drafted a letter in a neat hand. They had barely gotten to discuss the particulars before he had leaped off the couch and reseated himself at the desk, and Cassian couldn't tell if it was some kind of convoluted attempt to stall or not.

The insistent scratch of his pen stopped.

"What is it you expect me to do?" the hunter asked. His pen made an expanding blot of ink where it rested on the corner of his paper. He'd barely gotten past the initial salutation.

"I expect you to do what you do best," Cassian said. He ran his fingers over the top of a shelf of books. They bobbed up and down as they rode the unevenly matched spines. He pulled one free and flipped it open. "Fairy stories." He raised his eyebrows. "Research or for pleasure reading?"

"Does it matter?"

Cassian snapped the book shut and moved on, undeterred by the frown aimed at him. "It may. Who's to say?" He tugged another book from the shelf. This one was some kind of novel. “And as for what I want of you, I have good reason to suspect one of my own has betrayed me. Once you’ve discovered who, *you* will take care of them for me.”

“A vampire?”

“Yes, I did say as much earlier, didn’t I? I’m quite sure I did. And it seems very likely *my* betrayer is *your* would-be killer as well. The timing is rather convenient. Unless you have another theory on the matter. Do you have an assortment of other enemies to consider first?” He glanced at the hunter who only stared back as though dazed. “So, it stands to reason that if we take care of *my* problem yours will be solved as well. Which brings me back to my original question. How *did* you find where I was sleeping? You never answered.” The hunter opened his mouth, his expression clearly marking his intent to prevaricate even before a word passed his lips. “Please don’t lie to me.”

And there it was again, the little widening and then narrowing of his eyes, like a fire quickly tamped down, burn mark covered over with a rug in the hopes no one would notice. Cassian didn’t like to have to threaten people unless they deserved it, and it was debatable whether the hunter did—despite his previous attempt to behead Cassian while he was sleeping. Everything would go smoother if the hunter did his part willingly.

The hunter bit his lip. “I was assigned,” he said in a strained voice. His sigh seemed to drag all the air from his entire body, and he was left looking much smaller than before. He set aside his pen, frowning at the ink stain he'd made in his distraction. "There were reports of multiple deaths in the area—vampire related of course—plus missing livestock, so I was sent to investigate the cause."

"Someone told you I was there?"

"Not as such. Only the general area. I did the rest."

Cassian folded his arms over his chest, leaning back against the bookshelf, novel still clutched in one hand. He was considering keeping it. The gold decorating the edge of the pages was pretty. "Curious how I could be slaughtering my way through villages when I'd been asleep for decades, longer than you've even been alive. Generations." When the hunter turned a startled gaze on him, Cassian added, "I'm a very heavy sleeper."

"That's...not possible." He frowned, a little line forming between his brows before he turned back to his unfinished letter. "That can't be right. We had reports. There were at least a half dozen deaths." His voice faded away like early morning fog.

"Oh? Did you see all these bodies I'm supposed to have made?"

A shadow crossed the hunter's face. "No."

"Who gave you this report of my nefarious deeds?"

The hunter took up his pen again. He set a fresh sheet of paper on the blotter. "I need to finish this letter."

Cassian waited while he scratched away, line after line of pretty handwriting covering the page when he went to peek over the hunter's shoulder. He pulled the paper closer to his chest, all but lying atop the fresh ink to block Cassian's view. "Do you mind?"

"Another letter?" The first still sat unfinished on the desk, ink smudged by the hunter's restless shifting while they spoke. "Who are you writing to now?"

"Same letter," he said. His stiff shoulders said otherwise. "And headquarters. They should know more about the matter. If they can't tell me, I'll have to visit there myself." He stiffened as though realizing to whom he was speaking.

"Then I suggest you write your letter quickly. We have more to discuss." Cassian turned to the back of the house.

"Where are you going?"

He aimed a sly smile over his shoulder. "I'm hungry. Clearly this may take a while, and I see you have a conveniently placed wood. There must be something in it with blood. Unless you care to volunteer yourself." Cassian laughed. "Finish your letter."

If the hunter had any response, Cassian didn't wait to hear it before he was gone.

*

The woods were alive with all manner of creatures, and though not his favorite meal Cassian made quick work of a deer. The blood warmed him straight to the core before he leaped into the low-hanging branches of a tree and pulled out the novel he had tucked into his pocket on the way out of the door. The moonlight was pale, shining blue upon the cover and turning the gold edging almost to silver like clever alchemy. He held it up at an angle to watch the flash of reflected light. A pattern of faded gold leaves had been embossed on the spine too. He hadn't noticed that before. Cassian ran a finger over the barely there ridges of the pattern before he flipped the book open and began to read. Vampires were made for the night, or made *of* the night depending on who you asked, and the lines of text on the pages were perfectly clear. He would have been able to read them in all but the deepest of shadows.

From the dark we came, and to the dark we will return, was the saying. He took it with the modicum of skepticism that he did all legends. Vampires weren't human, and no matter what they looked like, they never had been. But they weren't pure, senseless shadow either. They existed somewhere in the liminal space between, until they too died. Then everything was the same. Or maybe not. He had no idea how the Fae worked. They were opposite sides of a coin and as much a mystery to him as vampires probably were to humans.

And what about *this* human? How much did he actually know?

Cassian turned a page, frowning.

He was starting to doubt whatever had compelled him to come to this place, to a tiny village leagues from any city. If there were any kin in the area, they were no doubt well hidden, perhaps even sleeping as he had been, and good luck to them if they were. With a hunter in their midst they may not stay that way for long.

He turned another page. This one came with an illustration featuring a little house atop a tall hill, and a tiny woman leaning out of the window in farewell. Flowers sprouted wherever her tears fell. Cassian snapped the book shut again and deposited it back in the pocket he had retrieved it from. He might present it to Erathel as a gift when he saw her next. His cousin had a fondness for such things.

Initially his plan had been simple.

When he fought the hunter months ago, he hadn't been thinking clearly. Newly awakened and filled with the sense of wrongness that came of finding a silver blade at one's throat and a bottomless hunger where one's stomach used to be would do that to a person he supposed. So, they had fought, and Cassian had escaped instead of finishing the job. A disgraceful end he had decided to rectify before he dealt with the fact that he was awake and didn't wish to be.

The hunter should have been dead by now. Cassian hadn't lied about the number of times he could have killed him, had underestimated if anything. Especially considering he had been watching for days already. Waiting. Biding his time as the hunter went cheerfully about town and greeted his tiny charges with pats on the head and surreptitious offers of sweets when their guardians weren't looking. Cassian had almost begun to suspect he'd found the wrong human before tonight because the only trait that grinning man seemed to share with his hunter was a long tail of black hair and the ability to distract Cassian from his plans.

The appearance of the shadow beast earlier had disrupted them even more. No one killed Cassian's hunter but him. And they certainly didn't kill Cassian's hunter in the midst of a crowd of humans, which had seemed the likeliest outcome. The beasts weren't known for their discretion. Tearing up human towns was bad for everyone. Too much of that and it wouldn't be lone hunters they needed to worry about. He might have lost his patience for kin politics, but that didn't mean he wished them all dead.

It felt good to dispatch the creature too. Like a small piece of himself returned. Maybe Cassian just felt better with blood on his hands, whatever color that blood happened to be. He preferred not to think too hard into it. One thought inevitably led to another and another, and before long, he was back in the morass that had sent him into the ground in the first place. Better not to chance it.

Cassian dropped from the tree and landed with a soft thud on the mossy forest floor below. Half the trees were bare this time of year, and the wind whistled through them like lonely voices. Fitting for his mood.

The hunter should have completed his letter writing by now. If he hadn't, too bad.

Trekking back through the woods was long and slow, hampered by so many trees growing so close together—there was something almost unnatural about how dense this forest was, he thought—so Cassian kept an eye on his footing as he walked. His muscles still protested all this movement, prepared as they were for sleep. He didn't disagree with them. Sleep was quiet. Sleep was dreamless. Sleep didn't have any opinions about anything.

His foot slid in a pile of moldering leaves, and Cassian caught himself against a tree, nails raking the bark in a long scar. He could have torn it straight from the ground if he wanted. Surely if anything justified a slight tantrum it was this situation.

The silence hit him all at once. It had been still before while he was hunting deer, but the usual kind of stillness that came with night and most of the world being asleep. He was well acquainted with the hush that fell over the world at night. This wasn't that. This was the silence of something lurking in the dark. If he wasn't the cause, something else was.

A branch snapped behind him, and Cassian waited, ears straining for the sound of further movement.

*

Belar fell asleep waiting for the vampire's return, curled into an uncomfortable curve on the couch, legs tucked close to his chest, and he woke stiff. Every muscle had knotted tight and set that way while he slept. His split lip stung. The scab tore open again as he yawned. He might have thought everything had been a dream if not for the wreck of his table and the freshness of his aches. Not the knees or the hips or the fire of numbness in his leg from how he'd been sleeping. Those were all the usual aches. But the stab along his ribs and the raw scrape of tender skin across his back—those were too fresh to be a dream. His throat felt scoured.

"Hello?" he whispered into the dark. His voice came out raspy.

No answer.

Writing and rewriting his letter had taken more time than he had expected, but he had finished and already posted it on its way to headquarters using the magic circle he had carved into the locked bottom drawer of his desk for correspondence. It should be waiting for Merriville whenever he cared to deal with his mail. With any luck, a response would be on its way back within hours. He'd also pinned a note to the outside of the door. He had no idea how long this affair might take, but he didn't want his students left wondering about his absence. The note declared that a business matter had called him away, and he would resume lessons upon his return. All of it technically correct. Then Belar had sat down to await the vampire's return or an answer from headquarters, whichever came first, and had apparently fallen asleep. He checked the floor by the front door. No return letter had slipped itself beneath it.

The lamp still glowed feebly, but even that had dimmed as the wick burned low. Outside the sky was velvety darkness. No birds with their early morning, pre-dawn chatter. Which meant sunrise was a long way off. Belar rose and turned up the lamp in the hopes of dispelling some of the darkness, but it did nothing for the chill wrapping his bones.

Something was wrong.

He'd often had that kind of feeling before—something which pointed him in the right direction, showed him a path where there was said to be none, showed him a *vampire* where others had found nothing—but he didn't even need it this time. Wrongness was sewn right into the fabric of this situation.

It was something the vampire had said earlier.

"Curious how I could be slaughtering my way through villages when I'd been asleep for decades, longer than you've even been alive. Generations."

It felt uncomfortably close to his last hunt. A vampire peacefully sleeping. Blue curtains hanging in a window. And not even a whiff of death about the place until Belar arrived to deliver it.

He glanced again at the door, willing a letter to arrive from Merriville. Still nothing.

Belar turned in the opposite direction, intending to pace, but found himself at the back door with his hand on the knob instead. The vampire had said he was going to feed. The thought made Belar a little sick. Not because of the blood. He'd seen plenty of blood, some of it his own, but more often belonging to the things he hunted. What bothered him was how, for a moment, he had imagined those hands and that mouth against his neck, his wrist, his pulse, and wondered what it would be like to let the vampire do what he would. To give in. What would he feel as those fangs pierced his skin? Would he struggle despite himself? He'd heard that a vampire's bite didn't have to hurt. Or if it did, the pain could be made delicious. Like the ache of a good fight. The way it pulled through him like putty and made him remember he was alive. He didn't mind that kind of pain at all.

As soon as he'd thought it, he pushed the thought aside. They might be temporary allies of a sort, but he doubted that would stop the vampire from tearing out his throat at the first opportunity. You couldn't trust a vampire. You couldn't trust Belar either. Perhaps that made them equals.

He pushed through the door and out into the cold night air. His breath fogged the air before the breeze carried it away. It was too early in the season for that. He should have had weeks more before it got this cold and his joints turned to rust.

There was no sign of the vampire in the yard. The wind rustled the leaves and the partially bare branches of the trees scraped together like inexperienced fiddlers, but nothing moved otherwise. That too was wrong. The owl that frequented the tree behind the yard was even more silent than a grave. Graves sometimes held vampires, and they were quite good at making noise when they wished.

The gate at the back of the yard hung open, caught on the forsythia bushes bordering the fence. Belar limped over to free it. The cold was already settling into him and making him regret coming out. He'd barely be able to move in the morning.

The latch clicked as he pulled the gate to. Perhaps the vampire had gone too far out into the woods and lost his way. Belar imagined it with petty pleasure. Lost and wandering until he was caught unawares by the dawn; the way his screams would be heard for miles as he withered in the sun.

Belar had no idea if it was even possible—vampires were weak to the sun, being of shadow as they were, but that day they had fought the sun had been up and yet the vampire had stood in it unharmed. He had no explanation for it even now.

The wind gusted in his face, and he tucked his arms around his body as he stared into the forest. His torn shirt wasn't much protection at all, and the shawl he'd pulled around his shoulders let the air pass through like a sieve. He wrinkled his nose. Beneath the familiar green smell turning over to crisp autumn mold was something else. Like smoke and rotten meat.

Belar turned. A shape pulled away from the blackberry bramble in the corner of the yard. There wasn't even a moment when he mistook it for the vampire.

Eyes like sores stared at him, darker even than the shadows surrounding them. They pulled in the weak moonlight and gave nothing back. The rest was a writhing mass, like eels swimming over each other in a tangle, though the overall shape was nearly human. Two arms. Two legs. One head. He thought it was only one head anyway, but it was so hard to focus on it for long that he couldn't be sure. Everything about the creature was wrong.

If you see one, run. And if you can't run, you're fucked.

There was no shame in running. Perfectly good people did it every day.

The beast made a noise like wet flesh and bones breaking before it hunched forward into a wolf-like crouch. Belar stood frozen.

The bell tolled from the town center, distant and echoing as it marked the hour, and the beast's head swung in its direction. Four chimes. Dawn wasn't going to save anyone, least of all Belar.

If you see one, run.

Belar grimaced. He dearly wanted to flee, but he couldn't let the thing run free in the town.

And if you can't run, you're fucked.

He had a knife in hand when the thing hit him. The impact knocked the breath from his lungs. The beast's weight landed on his chest, a sharpness like talons against his shoulders, pinning him in place. A great mouth gaped over him, more of that horrible stink washing out of it, so large that it was almost all he could see. An infinity of teeth and darkness waiting to devour him.

Belar drove his knife upwards. There was nothing. No resistance. He might as well have tried stabbing the fog. His hand and blade sank in to the wrist. The beast didn't even seem to notice.

Its bruising weight remained, but Belar couldn't connect. His fingers curled around clammy air instead of the monster's hide. His knife sliced the writhing smoke body to no effect.

He was going to die like this. He only hoped his students didn't come to call on him in the morning. He didn't want them to see whatever mess he left behind.

The claws at his shoulder raked skin as they flexed. *They* felt solid enough. Belar's eyes narrowed. It was worth a shot. He slashed at the clawed hand instead. This time there was the drag of flesh beneath the blade. The beast reared back with a howl. Belar rolled free.

"Good to know you're not all fog." His voice sounded muffled even to his own ears. Far away.

The beast rasped at him before it charged again. This time he was ready, dodging away at the last moment, knife out. Black blood colored the metal for an instant before it evaporated. He'd caught it along the side of the face. The beast tossed its head. A low growl rumbled in its throat. And when it turned its eyes on him again there was something different there. An almost human anger. The too-wide mouth curled in a snarl.

"And not just a beast either, it seems." The words fell from numb lips because the beast's next roar was followed with pain.

*

Cassian burst out of the woods just in time to hear the beast's bellow and see the tendrils of shadow spearing at his hunter, pikes a heartbeat away from impaling him.

It had been decades since he'd shifted over, but it came back as easily as moving through water. The rush of speed and fluttering of wind rushing over him, through him, as he became nothing but a shadow. Weightless. It felt like freedom. If he cried out, there wasn't enough left of him to make it audible. But the rush of speed—that was perfect.

He collided with the beast at full speed, shifting back as he did. Both of them tumbled end over end until they hit the fence. Cassian was back on his feet before the beast clambered up again. Its long-clawed feet gouged the grass as it turned back to him.

"Who sent you? Hmm?"

The beast cocked its head.

"I know you can understand me. Who?" He didn't expect an answer. For that it would need a tongue.

He didn't have a weapon this time, but that was only a minor problem. There were plenty of ways to kill something with only bare hands and the will. It was messier. And more time consuming. But he'd been asleep for seventy years. He could do with a stretch.

Cassian glanced behind him to where the hunter had lain sprawled in the grass.

He was gone.

Cassian spotted him a little ways from where he'd been. He had left a trail of leaves in his wake as he'd crawled across the yard. Their eyes met. The hunter smiled. The vicious glee in that look would have been worrying, but Cassian didn't have the chance because a second later the hunter raised a hand. Some kind of tube clenched in his fist. Then the yard exploded with light.

The beast screamed as the light ate through it, tearing flesh away in coal-black ribbons. Cassian threw up his arms to shield himself.

When the light had faded, the beast was gone—not dead—but gone for the moment. Cassian had fallen, knocked off his feet by the force of whatever the hunter had thrown. His hands and neck felt as raw as if he had scoured himself with steel wool. The hunter was still on hands and knees, bleeding from the shoulder where the beast had gored him. His smile hadn't faded at all.

"I wondered if that would work on you," he said in a weak, laughing voice before falling on his face unconscious.

Chapter Four

Soft.

There was softness beneath Belar's cheek. It wasn't the threadbare upholstery of his couch. He knew the feel of that without opening his eyes. This was a luxurious softness, and it came with the faint scent of something warm-spiced and rich.

He shifted, eyes still closed, and stretched the early morning aches from his muscles. They weren't there. Oh no. These were much worse. Instead of his usual aches he was met with pain so sharp and sudden he had to bite back a moan. The rest of it came back to him with a suddenness that bordered on nauseating. The vampire. The beast. The flare he had used to drive it away. By the time his head stopped spinning he was on hands and knees and looking around.

He was on a bed. Not his. The linens were saffron, the frame a massive construct of black-stained wood with mahogany drapes gathered to a single point in the ceiling overhead. The bed could have easily slept four with room to spare. A veritable seafaring vessel of comfort. He knew no one who could have fit—let alone afforded—such an immense bed in their house.

And the room...the room was... Belar squinted. The room was a blur. Without his spectacles he couldn't make out much of it except for the vague shapes of dark-framed portraits on the walls and burgundy paper in something that looked equally likely to be stripes as a floral design. A fireplace, the remnants of logs smoldering in the grate. An enormous chair like outstretched bat wings sat in the corner, casting a shadow so dense it was almost a part of the furnishings.

Of the three windows along the wall, the drapes of only one had been pulled back. The day was gray and dismal, rain and the smoke of a city's worth of chimney pots clogging the air so the sun barely penetrated the gloom outside, let alone in. There was no way to tell the time either. It was just as likely to be early morning as twilight on this kind of day.

A log on the fire crumpled, sending up a shower of ash. He jumped. The silence was eerie. No street noise penetrated the window glass. There wasn't even the tick of a clock. Quiet wrapped the room in a dense cocoon.

He was tempted to scream just to tear it apart.

Belar crept toward the edge of the enormous bed and looked down, ready for a monster to loom out at him and snatch at his ankles. It seemed like that kind of place. But he found nothing down there besides more dark wood flooring and a narrow mat woven in subdued browns and reds. He swung a leg down. His foot was bare. After that came another, belated realization. His shirt was gone and bandages wrapped his shoulder and around his back. There were nearly enough of them to qualify as a shirt in its own right. With his fingers he prodded at the white swath of gauze until he'd found each point of tenderness indicating an injury. They didn't feel extensive despite the needles of pain.

And he still had no idea where he was or how he'd gotten there. Finding out would require standing up.

He slipped off the edge of the bed. Then he kept slipping down, down, down. Belar cried out as he landed on his ass, from the cold of the floorboards as much as the jolt of pain. His elbow hit first, and his whole arm throbbed with numbness.

Across the room, the lock turned over with a snap, and the door swung in to reveal a short woman in a simple black dress standing in the gap. Her dark hair was cut across in a straight line just above the jaw. That and the way her large eyes drooped at the corners gave her the look of a slightly gloomy lampshade to Belar's blurry vision. "You're awake."

Belar squinted at her. From the dress, he guessed she was a servant of some sort. She looked human but there really was no way of knowing for sure unless she told him. "Yes."

If she thought it strange to find him lying on the floor, half dressed, she said nothing about it. "You're wanted downstairs." She bobbed a curtsy and retreated through the gap in the door.

"Wait!" Belar clawed his way back up onto the edge of the bed. His legs felt gelatinous, but they were getting better. "By whom am I wanted? And where is my shirt?" He glanced around the room, but there wasn't anything to see that he hadn't half-seen before. "And my spectacles?"

"I believe they were left on the bedside table for you. Do you need me to send someone in to help you dress?" Her expression didn't change, but he got the distinct impression she was laughing at him. He probably deserved it. "If that's all?"

She didn't give him the chance to answer before the door closed behind her. This time it was left unlocked. Apparently, he was free to come and go as he pleased now.

He found his glasses where she'd said, but even with them on, he couldn't find any sign of his shirt or his boots and had to settle for wrapping himself in a burgundy dressing gown he found slung over the side of the bed. He had missed it before, which wasn't surprising since the bed was immense. If he hid under the coverlet, no one would ever be able to find him. Depending on wherever this place turned out to be, that might still be his plan.

The longer he was awake, the more his shoulder throbbed. His fall had likely reopened the gash there. Without a mirror he couldn't check. He finger-combed the worst of the tangles from his hair and twisted it over his shoulder. Braiding would require another set of hands since he could barely lift his arms, and a brush, neither of which he had. He doubted his unknown host would care about the lack of propriety.

The hall was populated by a multitude of busts and sculptures on neat little wooden pedestals and row upon row of framed landscapes, their sunny pastel colors odd and bright against the dark wood paneling. Belar squinted down the hallway, but all the doors besides his were closed and no one appeared. Quiet voices emanated from somewhere below.

His feet sank into the dense carpet runner on the stairs as he descended. Everywhere he looked there was more of the same dark wood. Heavy draperies hung in all the spaces where windows might go, but when he pulled one aside, the window had been covered with shutters and a delicately curving but sturdy iron grate to discourage attempts at opening them. He let the curtain drop back into place, running his fingers along the damask papered walls around it. Even the copious lamps on polished side tables and the large, glittering pendant lamp hanging over the curved staircase couldn't completely dispel the gloom. He could have been in some kind of beautiful underground lair. So, he had a fair suspicion about whom this house belonged to even before the final stairs creaked beneath his feet and all conversation from below stopped.

A door yawned open like a hungry mouth ahead of him. The flickering orange glow of a fire reflected off the tile of the hallway, calling him forward with the promise of heat.

"Join us."

The voice was unfamiliar, the tone faintly amused, like a cat awaiting a new toy to bat around.

Belar strode forward. There was a fire, and he needed to know where he was besides. Coming here must have been the vampire's doing, which meant whoever lay inside that room probably didn't intend to kill him. In theory anyway.

It was a library, he found, as he stepped over the threshold, row upon row of books taking up every available inch of wall space that wasn't covered in more portraits, each a stark oval in a black wood frame with a tiny gold plaque affixed to the bottom. He couldn't see them all well enough to make out the features clearly, but an overall similarity to the shapes of the faces suggested they were related or—equally likely—the same subject over a long period of time. A vampirically long period of time. The light here was even more subdued than in the halls beyond, most of it emanating from the fire itself, and two flickering sconces set over the mantel. At the far end of the room, velvet draperies cascaded down the wall to pool on the floor. He wondered if he would find more shutters and iron bars there too if he tried to pull them back.

Two wingback chairs sat before the fire, both occupied, both by vampires. Sometimes it was difficult to tell a vampire from a human. Not in this case. At Belar's entrance, the vampires turned in unison to gaze at him with endless black eyes, the only color in them the amber ring of their irises.

Their skin was the same reddish brown as the vampire who had come to him, their hair the same glossy black though the one on the left wore hers braided with red and gold cord, and the one on the right wore his loose. It flowed like a black silk curtain, pulled over one shoulder, nearly down to his waist. The vampire on the right raised his glass to salute Belar—smiling in a way that made his fangs stand out—before he tipped his head back and drained the rest. The other studied him silently.

If anyone else was about, Belar couldn't see them.

Which left him alone with two unfamiliar vampires. Wonderful.

"Our cousin is busy. Don't worry. We don't intend to slaughter you in his absence."

"Planning to save that for his return?" Belar asked before he could stop himself.

But the vampire only laughed and tipped a little more wine into his glass from the decanter on the table set between the chairs. He swirled it before taking a sip, vulpine gaze fixed on Belar over the rim. "Possibly. If you ask nicely."

"You're being rude, Arakiel. Offer our guest a seat," the vampire woman said. Her voice was deceptively soft. It was like being caressed by a silk glove right before it slapped him. "My brother has no manners, forgive him. We get so few guests these days. And so unexpectedly too." She raised an eyebrow. "I am Erathel." Her head inclined in the slightest nod of greeting, but her hands stayed curled around the arms of her chair as though shaking or even touching was beneath her. He saw where all that regal arrogance came from.

Belar looked between Erathel and her brother. There was definitely a marked resemblance now that he was paying attention. A similar shape to the eyes, the long noses, the square jaws.

"Arakiel," said the other vampire, pronouncing his name as sharply as he did everything else. "And you...are human for some reason." He sounded amused.

"Do I *need* a reason to be?" Belar frowned at him only to realize the chair Arakiel had been occupying was now empty. A hand curled possessively around his shoulder. Belar stiffened. It didn't comfort him to see it was only Arakiel behind him.

"No, no. I just find it curious that he's taken to you so quickly. Though you are pretty enough." He leaned a cheek on Belar's shoulder, inhaling deeply. One of his hands finger-walked along the lapel of the dressing gown. "Wherever did he find you?"

Erathel didn't say a word. Her look was enough. Arakiel straightened with another sigh and steered Belar over to his vacated chair before pressing him down into the plush upholstery. A very full glass of wine was deposited in Belar's hand. Erathel didn't seem to have touched her own. It dangled from one of her long hands, another accessory like the cabochon ring on her middle finger. Her gold eyes met Belar's. He found it difficult to read any kind of expression in them. It was like looking into a scrying mirror, but instead of the future all he saw was endless night and time. So much time.

"How did I come to be here, wherever here is?" Belar asked. The vampire must have transported him, but the nearest city was miles and miles away without the use of his door. How long had he been unconscious?

"That was Cassian's doing," Arakiel volunteered, still leaning on the back of the chair over Belar's head, drumming his long nails against the fabric.

"He dragged you in our door late last night, covered in blood, and nearly unconscious himself. I had rather intended to ask *you* what had happened," Erathel added.

"Though it wouldn't be the first time Cassian had shown up that way. It's like the good old days again."

"Only you would consider dropping severed limbs on our doorstep 'the good old days,' Arakiel."

Belar blanched, but they ignored him.

"It was one. Singular," Cassian said from the doorway. "And only a hand at that. Hardly worth mentioning."

The dim light of the library left his features partially shadowed, but Belar saw the scratches on his face were already fading, bruises little more than hazy outlines against his brown skin. Even the ligature mark at his throat was nearly invisible. His unruly hair had been brushed and smoothed back from his face, slick and glossy with oil, and the loose shirt he wore left a long vee of skin visible at his chest. A square-cut ring on a chain hung in the gap, swaying slightly as he shifted.

Belar caught his breath at the sight of him. Deep in the pit of his stomach there was a faint flutter, a momentary sense of relief. He tamped it down. A known enemy was preferable to an unknown one, that was all.

"Have you been making my guest welcome?" Cassian asked.

Belar didn't think it was polite to say *no* when a vampire was perched on the back of his chair like a gargoyle. Especially since Arakiel had already demonstrated his ability to move fast enough to rip out his throat before he uttered a single word. "We're the best of friends already," he lied glibly.

"So I see."

Cassian glanced at Erathel who nodded slightly, a smile touching her lips for the first time before it disappeared again. Belar wasn't sure he hadn't imagined it. Then Cassian held out a hand. "You'll have to say farewell for the time being. We never got to finish our discussion. Time to rectify that."

*

Belar trailed in Cassian's wake out of the library and down more dark and unfamiliar hallways, their floors lined with thick runners that dampened every footstep and their walls lined with even more framed paintings. No more pastoral scenes like those upstairs. These ones were nightmarish landscapes that seemed to lean off the canvas in impasto swirls of burnt umber and crimson, their claw-branched trees ready to rake him bloody. They appealed to Belar in some strange way. "Where is this place?"

"Besides a house, you mean?"

"Yes, I know it's a house. But *where*?"

The vampire paused at double doors set with tinted diamond pane windows. He waved a hand for Belar to precede him before he followed and shut the doors again.

"Now we can speak freely," he said. He lounged against the door jamb, folding his arms over his chest. "Comparatively speaking. My cousins have incredibly acute hearing, so there's no telling when they are or are not listening."

Belar barely held in a gasp as he moved past the vampire. This wasn't another room as he had thought. It *looked* like a garden, but overhead the sky was a clear and starless curve of pink and purple dusk. Every corner of the space overflowed with plants: vines with long purple-black leaves or trumpet shaped flowers, evening primrose, white moonflowers studding trellises like glimmering coins. Belar wandered his way beneath a pergola festooned with more moonflowers, drooping black vines, and jasmine. None of this should have been growing this late in the year. He was fairly certain of that. And the view outside his bedroom window had been dismal and cold, but here it was warm. A gentle, summery breeze curled around his neck.

"It's a night garden. Bespelled," Cassian volunteered as Belar reached out to touch the yellow petals of another plant he had no name for. It was very possible the plant only existed here in this garden since a number of the plants looked like strange and distant relatives of those he knew. Enormous roses the size of saucers and tiny star shaped flowers grew in a dense cascade over the sides of planters. Dwarf trees in plaster urns hung heavy with pears and cherries. Belar reached up to pluck one before he thought better of it. Who knew if fruit in a vampire's garden was safe to eat. He might fill his mouth with blood instead of cherry juice. "A garden isn't much good if no one can enter it."

"I suppose so," Belar said. "It's beautiful."

"I'm sure Arakiel will be pleased to hear it. The garden is his. And as to where we are, it's Lysis. The city was the only place I could think of where we would both be safe for a while."

"Both of us?" Belar raised an eyebrow, pausing with his face half in the nearest flowering plant. It smelled very nice, whatever it was, like honey and the crystalline shimmer of magic. "Here? In a vampire's den? Two vampires," he corrected. "Not counting you."

Cassian grinned. "There's no place safer, believe it or not. My cousins are very dedicated to their hospitality."

"And you...carried me. All the way here. Somehow." There was no way around this fact that didn't end in Belar imagining himself as a swooning maiden draped over the vampire's arms. It was humiliating. Definitely humiliating. And he had missed it all.

"I can travel very fast when I need to. But there are limits." The vampire made no attempt to explain more. His eyes followed Belar as he moved on to inspect the next row of flowers. "Ah, and I almost forgot." He held up a familiar cream envelope. "I found this laying on the floor outside the library. Yours, I believe?"

Belar swooped over and snatched the letter out of his hands. He turned it over. "This seal is broken. How dare you open my mail?"

"It smells like magic, and I assume it's tied to your location somehow if it followed you all the way here. What a clever little delivery system you hunters have. I'd always wondered how you passed messages along. But, of course, I opened it. I had to be sure you hadn't decided to betray me after all. It's one thing to deceive me, but I can't have you attacking my cousins. They've done nothing wrong."

"That's debatable, I think." Belar unfolded the letter, eyes racing over the sparse text. When he had finished, he tucked the note into the pocket of the dressing gown. Merriville had been completely unhelpful, claiming no record had been kept of who reported the latest vampire attacks, and that he was too busy to look into it. Typical. Belar would have to do it all himself then. "I'll have to go in to headquarters." Lucky the vampire had accidentally brought him right to the city where headquarters stood.

Cassian nodded. "I assumed."

"From reading my mail."

"What is this clue my hunter is planning to search for? Perhaps I can help."

"I'm not *yours*. And you're not invited." He worried at his lower lip with his teeth.

Cassian made a noise of mock disappointment. "And here I thought we were finally becoming friends. I'm hurt." He reached out a hand, and Belar went still in anticipation of a touch that never came. The vampire plucked a rose from the bush beside him instead and lifted it to his nose. The ring he wore as a pendant flashed as it caught the light. "Pretty." He held the flower out to Belar. "You're going to have to trust me eventually if we're to work together."

That was exactly what he planned *not* to do. Especially not with the vampire looking at him like he was a meal waiting to be served up on a platter.

"A truce," the vampire said. "I swear I have no plans to harm you." There were no obvious conditions in the statement. Maybe if vampires were bound to their word like the Fae were, it would have given him some comfort.

Belar stared down at the rose. It was hard to discern the color in the dim light, but he thought it might be pink. Pink for innocence. That seemed ridiculous under the circumstances. Neither of them was the least bit innocent. “All right. A truce. Until this business is concluded, I promise I won’t try to kill you either.” He pulled the flower from Cassian’s fingers, mindful of the small but wickedly sharp thorns lining its stem. They were even sharper for how fine they were. He raised it to his nose. The vampire was right. It did smell sweet.

Cassian’s smile shifted ever so slightly into something darker. “Should we shake on it? Or kiss cheeks? Isn’t that what humans do?”

“No. I think we should not,” Belar said, but his treacherous imagination was already picturing that too.

“Aw. Pity. In that case, we have errands to run, your headquarters included. Which means unfortunately, you’ll need to dress in something a little more fitting than that dressing gown before we head out. Not that I’m not enjoying the sight. It suits you.”

Somehow Belar had forgotten about clothes and the fact that without the dressing gown he was down to a swath of bandages, a pair of torn and stained trousers, and his boots. It really wasn’t fitting for any kind of company unless he wanted to be arrested.

“We’ll leave at nightfall. And don’t worry. Arakiel will have something you can borrow.”

That was not at all comforting either.

*

Belar changed hastily, stripping off the dressing gown and dressing in the trousers, shirt, and double-breasted waistcoat in emerald silk Cassian had collected from among his cousins' things. He had no idea which pieces had come from whom, but he guessed by the delicate gold chains running between the buttonholes and the lace frilled cuffs that the coat at least belonged to Arakiel. It was disconcerting to know he had any taste in common with the vampire.

Outside it was only late afternoon, not evening as the sky over the night garden had suggested. Some of the gray haze had burned off, and by the time he'd finished dressing, the room was awash in eye-searing brilliance. It was like stepping out of a cave and onto the sun itself. He winced back from it.

Then he wedged a chair against the doorknob and crossed to the windows. The first one he tried opened easily, swinging outward without even a squeak of resistance. The three-story descent was considerable but could be eased by angling himself for a conveniently placed balcony on the second floor of the house. From there only a straight drop stood between him and the freedom of a bustling street. He almost felt guilty about how easy they had made it for him. He had climbed out of more difficult windows when he was still living with family.

Before he slipped over the casement and saw himself out, he just needed to do one final thing.

The rose really was pink fading to ivory in the center, fragile petals already bruised brown and wilting in the sunlight. Just like a vampire. It even drew blood like one of them. Maybe that was why Arakiel liked them so much. There had been rose bushes of all shades and varieties scattered through his garden.

Belar jabbed his thumb on one of the thorns and squeezed at the wound until the blood beaded up enough for him to smear it along the stem. There wasn't time to be dainty about it if he wanted a head start before the sun set. Then he took a deep breath. This was his least favorite part.

Unraveling his glamour took barely a second. There was no change in sensation to show it had happened, but he still felt bare. There had never been any freedom in being as he really was. He was so used to being *not* as he really was that it felt like stripping away a layer of skin instead of an illusion. A tool.

His hair fell over his shoulder and, even though he'd expected it, he flinched. Gone was the blackish hue, faded now to his natural blue-gray. He flicked his hair back with a frown. The only reason he'd taken off his glamour was to apply it elsewhere.

A minute later the rose was wrapped in his scent and his presence—his usual presence. He couldn't animate it in any way. The rose was still only a rose, but now it smelled like him and pulsed with the faintest echo of his heartbeat should any of his hosts be listening. It would have to do. He'd heard stories about what a skilled Fae glamour could accomplish but to him they were only that. Stories. His skills were nowhere near that level.

He tucked the rose in with the coverlet, wilting head laid over the pillow. His little co-conspirator.

Then Belar, Fae haired and pointy eared, let himself out of the window, dropped to the street below, and ran.

Chapter Five

The door to headquarters opened, and Belar let out a breath he'd been holding ever since he had woken up in an unfamiliar bed, in an unfamiliar room, in an unfamiliar house. It was good to be back among the glowing red-gold wood paneling and haphazard shelves of books. It was better to be back in his accustomed shape. He had pulled his glamour around him again as soon as he was far enough from the house to risk it, and he would be happy never to take it off again. Reality was stifling.

Belar only lingered a while in the multicolored twilight of the vestibule. The vampire was coming after him eventually and he planned to be elsewhere when that happened, truce or no truce. A bargain was only as good as the people who made it. Belar hadn't been able to hold his end for more than an hour. Odds were good that the vampire was going to be *very* unhappy with him when next they met.

The record hall was through a door and down a lift which was good since his knees didn't feel equal to a long flight of stairs. Between escaping out of windows, tension, and the weather conspiring together it was becoming an effort to ignore the pain in his joints. Maybe he really was getting too old for field work. Merriville and some of the others had been hinting at it for years already, but he couldn't deny the visceral need behind the work. To be out. To be doing. To be in the middle of humans living their lives. He might be safer behind a desk, maybe even more comfortable, but he wouldn't be *happier*.

There were only a few hunters in again today. Unfamiliar faces. Locals, he suspected from the way they were hurrying around to finish their work before dark. He didn't know most of the new people except by the traces they left around headquarters. None of them paid him any mind as he passed through.

A long bank of lights flickered to life overhead as he stepped out of the lift and started down the hall. Everything about headquarters was old and slightly worn around the edges, from the chipped marble busts of notable past figures to the cloudy glass sconces that hardly let the light through, but it was the closest thing he'd had to a home in over a decade. His cottage had a bed and a kitchen, he worked in the garden when the weather and his schedule permitted, but it wasn't the same as a home. No matter where he settled it always lacked something vital. He'd never been able to decide what it was. He only knew he felt its absence.

The record hall glowed brightly as he stepped through the door, rows of dangling bulbs illuminating the tall shelves full of books—most of them hand copied—and the card catalogs. His fingers glided along the rows as he looked for the section he needed. He had collected some of this information himself. Some of the bare spaces in the catalog were also his work, but no one needed to know that.

He had his nose in an old diary when a cough alerted him to a visitor. Belar turned the page and set the book down.

"You didn't come to see me when you got in," Merriville said.

When Belar had first come to this place, Merriville's brown hair had shown only the first streaks of gray like a threading of cobwebs. There wasn't much more gray now, only enough to look distinguished, but the lines around his mouth were deeper every time Belar saw him. The overhead lighting accentuated them and gave him the look of unfired clay slowly collapsing under its own weight. Normally when they spoke, it was in his office or the main room so Belar hadn't noticed that before.

"Ah, sir. I was just about to head your way. Though I'm surprised to see you in the office so late. Your message was hours ago. I expected not to find you."

"I know you keep late hours," he said with a twitch of his mustache. He took in the books arranged around the table. Out of long habit Belar had collected an assortment, a holdover from the days when he'd cut his hours of hunting research with inquiries of his own and buried the evidence beneath mountains of unrelated reading. Not that any of those searches had ever amounted to much. Some things even he couldn't find. "I don't recall assigning you to anything new. You're supposed to be on leave, aren't you?"

Belar gathered everything back into a stack, swearing silently. "You didn't and I am. I was just looking into a legend I heard the other day. Seeing if it might necessitate an official hunt."

Merriville hummed. Then he pulled his watch from his pocket and flipped it open in a meaningful way. "I have a few minutes before I turn in for the night. Accompany me to the door, and you can tell me all about it." Merriville snapped his watch shut. It sounded rather like Belar's last nerve giving way. "Or shall we discuss that note of yours? Something about a mistake on a hunt, was it? Which hunt did you mean?"

Belar stood to follow, pressing his lips tight to stifle the groan that threatened to escape. *Oh stars*, sitting so long had been a bad idea. "Midsummer. To the north, around Sineschel." When Merriville continued staring uncomprehendingly, he added, "The vampire."

"Ah. Yes, yes. The failed hunt," he said, rocking on his heels in a way that made his shoes squeak against the tile floor while he waited for Belar to pull open the lift so they could enter. "First time you've ever disappointed. That was a surprise."

Belar smiled. "Yes, it was," he agreed. Smiling. "For me as well."

They rode up to the next floor in silence, and then Belar yanked open the gate so they could step out of the lift and Merriville could be on his way. Anything to be done with this conversation.

"Do you recall who put that hunt into the queue?" Belar asked. His smile was beginning to hurt. In the cheeks mostly and at the corners of his eyes.

"Hmm...no. I can't say I do. All that paperwork should be archived now though if you closed it out. Why? You said something about a mistake? What kind of mistake? You claimed to have *lost* the vampire. Did you find it again?"

"No, no. Nothing like that. Filing error," Belar lied. "I was only thinking of correcting it. For the records."

They were to the doors then. The main floor had cleared out, all the lights inside offices dark. It must be later than Belar had realized. Merriville retrieved his topcoat from a rack by the door and shrugged into it with his back to Belar, who took the opportunity to massage the feeling back into his face. "Ah, I wouldn't worry about it then. There will be time for that later. Rest while you can. You've been looking a little weary."

"I will. Thank you. Sir."

After he'd collected his hat as well, Merriville reached for the door. "After you."

"I'll be off in a moment. I left all those books unshelved. I don't feel right leaving them for someone else to put away," he said with mock disappointment.

Merriville shrugged and was on his way with a wave and another admonishment about working too late. "Even in the city it isn't entirely safe to be out so late, you know. Too many beasties slip through."

Belar's smile returned full force. "Thank you for the concern. You be careful as well, sir."

When he was sure Merriville had gone, he turned back the way they had come. He hadn't checked his archived files yet, but he meant to do just that.

"Such charming company you keep."

Belar gasped as his eyes picked out the vampire standing beneath a stained-glass window. The low light from the nearby sconce gilded his dark hair and left his eyes shadowy pits. He looked no angrier than usual. Actually, he didn't look angry at all. He looked...amused. That was almost more disturbing than if he had attacked Belar on sight. Maybe he really was sincere about this truce of his.

"You followed me," Belar accused. Always better to stick with the facts.

"The door was open. And you're hardly one to talk. You lied to me first. It took me an age to pick up your real scent again after that little stunt of yours. But thank you for the blood. You were delicious." He grinned.

"You—"

"Licked it off the rose, yes. It was like a beautiful little snack, and you weren't using it anymore. That makes it fair game."

Heat crept up Belar's collar before he remembered to be angry. "You can't be here. Get out."

"Why? The place seems to be empty, and we have a truce. That makes us allies," he purred. "Have you found anything?" He raised his eyebrows, seeming legitimately curious.

"Not yet. I was headed back down to continue researching."

"Excellent. I will assist."

"No, you will not."

"It would be faster to search together, don't you think? And anyway, if I go back now, Arakiel will force me into joining in his latest obsession. I can't bear it."

"If it will cause you physical pain, I'm even more in favor. Go. Do that. With my blessings."

Cassian was at his side as Belar started away. His steps were like a whisper against skin. He'd dressed in a long, draped coat that swirled around him as he moved, the front a masterpiece of tiny gold buttons and embroidery in ruby thread that must have taken weeks to complete. Belar wondered if it belonged to Cassian or if it had also come from his cousin's closet. "It seems like a waste when there are so many more enjoyable ways of inflicting pain. Paddles for instance."

"I'm sure I have no idea." A blush crept up out of his collar.

"Really? Would you like to?"

Belar swallowed around the lump in his throat and kept his face carefully blank. He had never been so happy to see the door to the archives in his entire life. And he was not considering anything the vampire had just suggested. Almost definitely not. "I have *work* to do. That's what you hired me for, isn't it? To work?" He yanked open the door. Unfortunately, it didn't hit the vampire as it closed.

"Well, well," Cassian breathed as he took in row upon row of files. "Someone *has* been busy. Do you not think it a little arrogant that humans feel no qualms meting out their own justice on vampire kind without oversight? To say nothing of whatever else you lot get up to."

"If they're harming humans, it's only right that the humans should protect themselves, so no, I don't think so at all. And how are you any different? Have you suddenly developed scruples about assassinating your opponent?" Belar raised an eyebrow.

"Oh no. I still want you to kill them. Preferably in a memorable way that will relieve me of all suspicion. I recognize that this may be a difficult order but do your best."

Belar turned away to the card catalogs, ignoring the stack of books he'd been reading earlier. He didn't want the vampire to know what exactly he'd been researching. There had been no reference at all to previous vampires impervious to the sun, and he'd only just started looking into Cassian's cousins when Merriville had interrupted him. The rest would have to wait until he was alone. In the meantime, he could find his reports and see if there was anything he had missed there.

Merriville's smarmy tone rang again in his ears, speaking about failed hunts. He was never going to live that down. A perfect record, ruined.

The vampire's voice interrupted his brooding. "What is it you're searching for?"

"Nothing."

He appeared at Belar's shoulder again, shadow falling over the contents of the drawer. "Cards. What do they do?"

Belar slapped his hand when he reached for one. "It's an index. Don't touch. You'll get them out of order. I need to find your file, and to do that I need to find it in this card catalog first."

While he searched, the vampire conducted a search of his own, riffling through the nearest bank of shelves. He tugged out a book and opened it. This was becoming a habit with him.

"Please leave that alone." It was too late to stop him of course, since he'd already done it, but at least this way Belar could accurately claim he had attempted to stop the invasion.

"This says Dismas on it," Cassian said, spreading the pages open with one large hand so Belar could see. The name had been written in an elaborate hand, ink faded with age. Alongside that, someone had added a neat block of explanatory text detailing the circumstances leading to the organization's possession of the book. Belar already knew everything in it by heart.

“Yes.”

“Dismas the vampire?”

Belar paused in his search and inserted a finger into the row of cards to keep his place. He stared at the vampire over the top of his spectacles. It left him blurry at the edges, but Belar had always found the look particularly good for communicating his displeasure and he was *very* displeased. “Yes. The journal was recovered along with a number of other artifacts during a hunt. Do you have a problem with that?”

“On the contrary, I’m glad he was dealt with. He was a fiend. And now I don’t have to worry about him turning up for another attempt at treason.” He paused. His mouth drooped into a slightly baffled pout. “Though I suppose it’s no longer any business of mine either way.”

“Good. Then put the book away. I don’t want to see it.”

Cassian hummed thoughtfully, flipping a few more pages in the book before replacing it on the shelf where he’d found it.

Belar returned to his cards. Only after a moment did the full meaning of what Cassian had implied sink in. “Who exactly *are* you?” Belar asked.

“I’ve already told you my name.”

“That was your cousins actually. And you’ve told me nothing else.”

"You didn't ask so I assumed you already knew. Am I not in your library somewhere? How disappointing."

Belar's eyes narrowed. "No. I don't know. And at the moment, I still have no idea how I'm to locate your assassin if these files prove unhelpful. I need more information," he said, trying a different angle. "Entertain me."

"*You're* my assassin, lest we forget."

"Not yet I'm not," he grumbled. Belar bent over the cards again, walking his fingers over the tops as he searched for his own name.

Cassian laughed lightly. "Very well. You've made your point. And I'm rather looking forward to finding out if I'm in one of your books somewhere." He touched one gloved hand to his shoulder and bowed. "You may know me better by my title. Former Right Hand to the sixth princess of the shadow realm. Leya still reigns last I checked, but I stepped down. In a manner of speaking. I'm sorry, I don't have a calling card, so you'll just have to take my word for it."

The card drawer slipped from Belar's fingers.

The vampire's eyes followed the fluttering of cards all the way to the floor. A small, complicated smile touched his lips. "Ah. So you *have* heard of me."

There wasn't much known about vampire society. They'd had to piece it all together from scraps, journals, decades-old stories left behind by people who had run afoul of them. Even the creation of vampires was shrouded in a dense layer of myth. They weren't human now. That much was clear. But if they ever had been, no one knew. The vampires certainly weren't telling. They didn't interact with the human world except to occasionally feed on and kill them—neither of which was helpful for information gathering.

That had always been the supposition anyway. Belar was having a harder time believing it after seeing Erathel's and Arakiel's house, right in the middle of the city, the immense structure like a thumbed nose at the hunters, who had settled their headquarters only blocks away. And if they were there, so obviously something beyond humanity, who knew how many others were lurking nearby? All of it right beneath their noses.

The only thing they *did* know about vampires was the ruling hierarchy, thanks to a recovered book penned by some kind of vampire scholar. The stories were hard to follow, much of the context lost, but it was a base. A base suggesting an entire tower of things they didn't yet know. And all of it just as shadowy as they themselves were.

A circle of seven princes and princesses who'd split the dark between themselves. There were even whispers that the seven were the original vampires. Eldest of their kind. The first vampires who stepped out of the shadows and took flesh. It sounded too fantastical to be believed, but there were references going back centuries.

Belar had no idea how much was absolute truth, but the vampire had called himself the Right Hand. He'd seen that term before, while researching in this very room.

"*You're* vampire aristocracy."

"Former, and not exactly. I'm nothing now since the terms were that I leave with only my name. And not even the whole thing. I would rather not go into it all if you don't mind." Cassian's eyes shifted toward the door. "Do you hear that? Someone is coming."

"Don't change the subject—"

"They're headed this way. But if you don't mind them seeing me here, with you, I have no objections."

Chapter Six

Belar snarled—actually snarled—before lunging for Cassian. Then, fists wrapped in his lapels, the hunter dragged him into the nearest row of the labyrinthine shelves and around a corner, a hand covering his mouth. A knife, Cassian noted, was now pressing into his side just below the ribs. He hadn't been so amusingly manhandled in a long while. "Don't make a sound. Stay here," he hissed in Cassian's ear. He pulled away and stalked back toward the door. On guard, though the knife in his hand disappeared up a sleeve like a clever trick.

The door creaked inward. At the sight of whoever stood there, he relaxed. "What are you *doing* here, Marta? You scared me half to death."

The woman laughed as she stepped further into the room. Cassian could track her by the faint scent of her toilet water and the heady smell of blood beneath. She had an open cut somewhere. Recent. "I'm just back from some digging and saw the lights. Anyway, I could say the same of you. You're supposed to be out of rotation. This loitering is getting as bad as Horace. Both of you need to find something else to do with your free time." Her tone asked the question her words didn't.

"I got restless. Couldn't sleep."

She made a noise of understanding. "So you came all the way here. When you're on leave for the season. In the middle of the night. I see." A pause. "Who is that you've got with you?"

"What?"

Cassian had to hold in a huff of amusement. The hunter really was a terrible liar under pressure. It was a continual surprise. And a delight. He hadn't been this entertained in at least a century and a half, maybe more.

"You act like you're the first to sneak a date into the archives to show off. Come off it, Belar. You guarded the door for me plenty in the old days. I'm not going to give you away."

"It's not—"

"Whatever. It doesn't matter to me one way or the other." She came another step closer and Belar took one back. "Don't I even get to meet them?"

"No." Then, with a malicious look in Cassian's direction and a smile that was all teeth, he added, "They're not decent."

The comment was met with a raucous laugh. "You sly little thing. You do fast work." She sounded impressed. "Next time then. And maybe lock the door if you don't fancy a round of exhibitionism with your trysting, hmm? Nice almost meeting you, whoever you are," she called.

Belar stood guard over the end of the aisle until the door shut behind her and then hurried over to turn the lock as she'd instructed.

Cassian sauntered out of his hiding place. “I’m indecent, am I?” He didn’t hate the sound of that.

“Completely,” Belar said in a flat voice. It didn’t stop his gaze from finding Cassian’s lips. “Now help me clean this mess up. We can’t be here all night, or someone will get suspicious.”

*

Belar ignored the discomfort in his knees as he crawled around the floor collecting cards and handing them off to the vampire to slot back into the drawer where they belonged. He rather thought their roles should have been reversed. Having the man on his knees for him was only fair after everything that had happened. The image crystallized before he could prevent it, flooding him with heat straight down to his toes. It was all Marta’s fault for putting the idea into his head.

He’d never been one for casual sex, or casual anything really. Not when he was a patchwork of secrets in need of keeping and he couldn’t remember the last time he’d felt more than a passing desire. That was the thing about being demisexual. Sex was so rarely the first or even tenth thought in his mind. Even if he enjoyed it. Getting it was like some indecipherable dance. Most of his attempts in the past had been circuitous affairs built up over months, sometimes even years, and often culminated in one or the both of them losing interest before any clothes were ever removed. Generally, they didn’t make it within a mile of a bedroom.

He knew it was different for most of the other hunters. Marta was right. Belar had watched the door for her on many a night while she had women on this very floor. She wasn't the only one. But this was the first time Belar had ever considered trying it himself. Maybe it was so suddenly finding himself the prey of another's hunt. It brought every impetuous urge he had to the surface and made him wonder if a single bright burning moment of pleasure might be worth it. Just this once.

There was no shame in it. Their work was meant to be secret, but it was also an unspoken agreement among the associated hunters that they might as well enjoy themselves in whatever ways they saw fit while working a largely thankless job that was liable to kill them without warning. Heroes only got to enjoy their laurels while they were alive to do so, and as long as everyone cleaned up their own mess, no one complained.

"You're very silent," the vampire said and Belar dropped the cards he'd collected a second time as he jumped.

Belar cleared his throat. "I was thinking on something."

Cassian held out one kid-gloved hand to receive the next batch of cards. Each little card went into the drawer with a decisive tap, underscoring his own patient silence.

"I'm not going to tell you what it was."

"You're incredibly bad at cooperation, has anyone ever told you this?"

"It's private and you don't get to berate me when you didn't even tell me who you were. Didn't *you* think that piece of information might have been useful in figuring out who wants you—us—dead?"

"To be honest, I thought you were lying about not knowing who I was. Do you really go around stabbing *every* vampire in a tomb that you find? Without even learning their names? That seems frightfully rude."

"I told you already, I did my *research*," Belar snapped, all his earlier fantasies dissolving like spun sugar. "We don't get a list of names and you didn't exactly nail a plaque to your door to announce yourself. The report said you had been snatching children and livestock for a span of months. Local gossip supported it. Was I supposed to wait for you to wake up and ask for a calling card before I dealt with it?"

Cassian recoiled. "Children? I would never. I might have eaten a few of their sheep, but that was ages ago before I went to sleep, and I didn't even enjoy it. Sheep's blood is ridiculously gamey. But I snatched no children."

For some reason Belar believed him.

He gathered the last of the cards and Cassian took his hand along with them, pulling Belar to his feet. His thumb stroked over the sensitive skin on the back of Belar's hand. A gentle touch at odds with the situation. This close he could smell the vampire's scent again like woodsmoke and spice. He snatched his hand back and tugged his gloves back on.

"So, you're practically royalty."

Cassian made a face. "No. If you want that you'll have to look elsewhere. As I said, I gave up any status I had when I went to ground. I thought I gave up my enemies along with it, but it seems I was mistaken."

Belar held up the card he'd kept back, the list of his records scrawled across the bottom and the back in cramped writing, dates and shelving locations in neat lines. "Let's see what the report says about that."

*

As it turned out, the report only gave him more questions. Belar had been over the whole thing numerous times two months earlier as he tried to make sense of what had happened, enough that he had nearly memorized its contents.

"This report is wrong," Belar announced after flipping through the sheaf of papers for the fourth time.

"Of course it is," Cassian said. "It says I fed on children. I'm not a monster."

"There are those who would disagree with you on that last point," Belar said, "but that's not what I meant. This isn't the report I filed after I lost you."

"It isn't? How do you know?" Cassian leaned over his shoulder and Belar stiffened as the vampire's scent filled his nostrils again. He was becoming uncomfortably fond of it. Maybe this was another tactic to ensnare prey.

Belar shifted slightly away. If only he didn't need to *breathe*.

"Someone has altered this. I'm sure of it." He jabbed a finger at several lines of text. "The type bar on our typewriter has a distinctive defect on the lowercase *H*. This *H* is wrong. I'm also sure the initial report was longer by several pages. The documentation was solid. There was even a map to your suspected resting place—it was wrong, completely wrong, but it was definitely there. I returned it with my corrections. It's now gone."

"You're very proud of yourself, aren't you?"

"Do you have *any* idea how many hours of research I put into locating you? There was a reason I drew the report. No one else could have tracked you. If they had tried, you would still be tucked away in your tomb dreaming about virgin's blood or whatever it is vampires dream of..."

"You have a very skewed opinion of my people," Cassian said, one finger coming under Belar's chin and tilting his head up until their eyes met. His eyes darkened, pupils nearly swallowing the amber ring of his irises. When he spoke next, it was barely a whisper. "But when I drink, I prefer it to be freely given. There are plenty willing to offer what I need. They come to me on their knees, begging, and I give them all the pleasure and all the pain they could ask for. They take it with a smile on their lips." He cocked his head, gaze raking over Belar. Around them the room seemed to dim to a faintly pulsing black where only he and his eyes and his mouth were visible. They were so completely alone. For the first time in a long while, Belar felt vulnerable. “And when I’m done, they say *thank you.*”

Belar swallowed hard, choking a little.

Slowly, the vampire moved back, releasing his hold on Belar as he leaned a hip against the table. His mouth quirked up in a crooked smile that showed the tip of one fang. “Also, I’m loath to disillusion you, but vampires rarely dream. We have to satisfy all our fantasies while we’re awake.” He sifted the length of Belar’s ponytail through his fingers, the slight tug making Belar shiver, though he didn’t pull away. “Any other questions?”

Belar turned back to the report, fingers tightening on the paper as he fought the tingles slithering down his spine. If he pretended they weren’t there, maybe they would go away. And then he could stop trying to pretend he didn’t enjoy them. “You miss my point. Someone has been here, not once but several times, planting false reports. If yours was faked, then who knows how many others might have been?” All at once it dawned on him. He felt sick. “Shit. I need to check something.”

Belar stumbled out of his chair. He yanked one portfolio after another, all his most recent hunts, spreading them out across the table like a terrible secret. There were only five from this year thanks to the weeks he had spent researching each. He’d been too busy to take on anything else. Any other year there might have been as many as two dozen. Five felt like a mercy.

The thickest, the ongoing spate of hauntings in a southern town, was free of tampering as far as he could tell. No incorrect Hs. No missing pages. And he had seen the effects of the ghosts with his own eyes, felt their attacks. He quickly set that file aside.

The file on a creeping sickness that turned out to be perfectly natural was equally un-noteworthy.

Which left two others besides Cassian's. Both vampires. He began with the most recent. Flipping back the cover of the file turned his stomach. He already knew what he would find there, and he didn't want to see it. He didn't want to be right.

And yet...

Papers exploded out of the file as it hit the wall. He snarled in wordless rage.

He leaped up and paced so he wouldn't be tempted to throw the rest of the files, the books, anything he could get his hands on. Cassian followed him with his eyes. It had been a naive hope to expect the culprit might have signed their name to the crime, but finding the opposite—a file completely wiped clean—disturbed him even more by what it suggested.

"Who were they?" Belar demanded. "Who did I kill?" He didn't need to check the third file. He remembered it as being similar to the others and he couldn't bear to see the signs a third time and realize he had missed them. It didn't matter that he'd had no reason to suspect at the time. It didn't matter that he'd had altruistic motivations. All that mattered now was finding whoever was responsible and putting a knife in their heart. It seemed like the only sensible answer to the problem.

Cassian walked over to collect the papers Belar had thrown. He gathered them back into a stack and tapped it on the tabletop to straighten them before he set it aside. "I don't know. I suppose I'll have to read these reports of yours. But I would rather not do it here." He glanced toward the narrow-slit windows high up the walls. "The sun will be up soon."

"We both know it doesn't affect you," Belar said dryly, feeling his anger fade the slightest bit. It was still a simmering flow that made his head throb, but it was better. "You don't need to pretend."

The vampire smirked. "Just because it won't kill me, doesn't mean it doesn't hurt quite a lot."

"And why *doesn't* it kill you?" Belar threw himself against the nearest wall and folded his arms over his chest. "Personal curiosity. Not for my reports."

"Oh? Are we sharing information now? When did this happen?"

"Around the time I found out someone has been using me as their personal executioner without my consent."

"I can work with that. But I meant what I said. We need to leave. If someone has been acting through you, then all the more reason to leave this place. It isn't safe."

Belar hated that he agreed.

Chapter Seven

Belar looked hollow, as though everything that made him up had been transported to some other place and Cassian had been left with the walking husk that remained. He'd barely even argued as Cassian tucked the stack of portfolios into his coat and led them back to the house. Now he sat in a chair before the fire and stared into the flames. He was close enough that the heat had turned his cheeks a fierce pink, but he seemed not to notice.

Erathel and Arakiel had disappeared to their daytime resting places. They moved rooms frequently—Arakiel claiming boredom but the more likely reason to make them harder to locate—so Cassian was unsure exactly where they were, but he sensed the flutter of their presence within the walls of the house. It was like a slow-beating heart beneath his palm. He had missed that. The knowledge that others were near. His long repose had been silent and still until the hunter had interrupted it. Just the faint scrabbling of insects and the slow drip of time to keep him company. The quiet made it easier to slip away for long periods, whole years eaten up between one breath and the next. He hadn't slept since.

There was an awful lot of time to fill when one didn't sleep, he was finding.

An hour ticked by while Cassian read through the neatly organized files he had stolen, including his own. Beside him, the hunter slowly slumped in his chair as he fought to stay awake.

"You know, there *is* a bed upstairs of which you're welcome to partake. The room is yours for the duration of this truce. I trust you won't even attempt to sneak out the window this time," Cassian said without raising his eyes from the paper in his hands.

It was terribly morbid. All of this was. Reading about his own attempted murder. Trying to piece together the identities of the others who had been killed based on their location and a few vague descriptions. He probably should have minded it, but it was so close to his old work that there was a strange comfort in it. A symmetry.

"There'd be no attempt about it if that's what I wanted to do," Belar said in an irritable mutter. It sounded like he might already be asleep.

"Yes, yes."

"I mean it. I've been sneaking out of houses since I learned to walk. The only reason I'm still here is so I can find whoever is responsible for this. I want to put my knife through their heart. Repeatedly." He sat up, hands clenching into fists on the armrests. "I have never been so *angry*." He turned on Cassian. "You've been reading forever. Do you know who those vampires were or not?" he demanded.

"I have a suspicion. Though it doesn't explain why they—or I—have been targeted." He dropped his chin into his hand. "The woman fits the description of Revia, what little I remember of her anyway. We met and spoke only a few times, thrice at most. She wasn't often in company. Kept to herself except for brief appearances for the Long Night and such." He toyed with the corner of the topmost paper as he tried to call up any substantial recollection of her, but every memory he had was nearly a century old already. So much time for things to fade. Had they ever spoken or only sat on councils together? He thought they must have exchanged a few words over the years, but try as he might, he couldn't remember when or what about, could only remember her face twisted into a frown, white hair pulled up into her ubiquitous knot atop her head. Cassian folded everything back together and set it aside on the table beside the decanter. He didn't drink or he might have been tempted to partake of a glass. It seemed like an occasion for it. "The other was Philomen. He was known to have gone to ground in that area. He liked being close to the water when he slept. Said it was peaceful."

"I see."

"I didn't know either of them particularly well. We weren't friends. They were both elders, or nearly so, and I was busy elsewhere."

"But you'd met them."

Cassian nodded. "Philomen a little more frequently, but yes. He was a scholar of sorts, so we had dealings that way. I'm not sure why the three of us would have been targeted aside from the fact we were all sleeping. We weren't even in the same areas. As you know." He tipped a look at Belar again since he'd gone silent.

His expression was roughly what Cassian had expected. It really was a wonder he didn't catch fire.

They sat in near silence, Cassian trying to remember anything about the two vampires that might prove useful, Belar making small angry noises beside him. It was almost companionable.

"Have there been any other missing vampires?" Belar asked suddenly. "You were sleeping which made you easier to kill but more difficult to find. What about others who were awake?"

An interesting idea. Though he had no way of knowing himself. In the roughly two months he'd been awake, Cassian had spent most of his time feeding to make up for seventy years' lack and then hunting down his hunter. He hadn't been back to society at all unless one counted his cousins. Perhaps it was time to change that. "I don't know, but there is someone who might. Luckily she's local." Cassian smiled as the hunter's face was transformed by suspicion. "We can go there tonight and say hello."

*

"Where are you taking me?" Belar's voice dripped with suspicion.

He'd slept fitfully in the too-large bed, like the very absence of anything around him was cause for concern, and had woken again in an agony of tense muscles and old bruises. There was a *reason* he didn't work once the weather turned cold. Irritation buzzed beneath his skin, only slightly lessened by the tray with a cup of coffee that had been delivered to his room upon his waking, a reminder that it had been over a day since he ate. Millicent's house was years ago already. And the coffee was served black and in a teacup so expensive and delicate it might shatter in his hand, only underscoring the fact that he was in a very different place now.

Now they wandered the city at night, Cassian slithering from one shadow to the next as he avoided the puddles of gas lighting. Somehow, he made it seem as though it was a perfectly normal thing to do. He cast a look back at Belar who lagged helplessly in his wake on the unfamiliar streets. He hadn't lived within city limits in over a decade, not since he'd earned his door linking spell, and now when he visited headquarters it was a trip straight there and then immediately home. He didn't linger. Time and darkness had rubbed out all his old familiar landmarks. He felt like a hapless tourist waiting to have his pocket picked.

"We're visiting a friend, as I said. If there's anything to know Marisol will know it. She's the most well-informed person this side of the channel. Trust me."

"Never."

Belar shoved his hands deep into his pockets and tried to keep his pace even so his limping wouldn't show. Or maybe the vampire would take it as a simple affectation if he did notice. There were plenty who swaggered around for no other reason than the style of it. He certainly wasn't going to explain one way or the other.

"Why are you doing this?" Belar asked, eyeing Cassian sidelong. The vampire had dressed in a midnight-blue coat with flared tails this evening and it made him look like some kind of magnificent and lethal bird. Belar was starting to enjoy looking at him and not just for the pleasure of his impeccably tailored silhouette either. That didn't hurt. But it wasn't the only reason. "I know why *I'm* doing this." He held up a hand to tick each reason off on his fingers. "Firstly, because you threatened me. Secondly, because I don't appreciate being maneuvered into killing under false pretenses. Thirdly..." He trailed off, not even sure what he'd meant to say there. That he felt guilty for having a hand in this, even accidentally? That he'd tossed and turned this morning as the truth pressed down on him? He had suspected. Maybe not at first, but later, and he'd gone through with it anyway. He'd become a hunter to protect people—humans specifically, but any who were in need, he supposed. To be useful even if no one outside of a select few ever knew about his actions. It was a sort of trust. And now it was gone. He cleared his throat. "So why are you?"

"Aside from the obvious?"

"Aside from the obvious. You don't even seem particularly upset that someone wants you dead. Or you hide it *very* well. So why?"

There was no answer for a very long time, just the low hum that seemed to signal Cassian was thinking about something. "Do you know why vampires go to ground? Generally, I mean."

Belar shook his head. Even after years of hunting them, he barely knew anything about vampires. No one did.

Cassian's eyes were dark. His pace slowed, lingering between one slip of shadow and the next. He didn't look at Belar. "Too much of anything can become a bad thing, including life. So we sleep. That's why I slept. Perhaps I'm wrong and others feel differently, but I stripped out of my old life like a soiled suit and tossed it aside because I was tired of who I was. I didn't consider what it would be like to wake up to a world that had moved on and realize I was the only one who didn't. So, in answer to your question: I don't have anything else to do. Or anywhere else to go. But I woke up to an axe at my throat and I want to know *why*." His voice lowered to a growl on the last word. That was the voice Belar remembered from the first time they had fought, the vampire shrugging off his attacks like water, one question ringing in the air between them. *Why? Why? Why?* That had unnerved him more than anything else. One word uttered like a prayer to an angry god.

He'd always wondered what the vampire was really asking. Now he knew.

"I see" was all Belar could think to say.

"You don't. But you may in time."

They had begun walking again without Belar even realizing, as though the vampire was a magnet drawing him along, and now when he glanced around Belar had even less of an idea where they were. None of the street names were familiar, the facades of the buildings, nothing. Even the gas lighting looked faintly off, as though he was viewing it from behind a fine curtain of lace.

"Here we are," Cassian announced. All trace of his earlier mood was gone and now he sounded cheerful again.

Belar's suspicion spiked alarmingly. He didn't even have a chance to read the name painted on the large storefront window before he'd been dragged to the recessed doorway. "We're friends here. You're not a hunter, you're my guest," Cassian whispered, bending to speak beside Belar's ear again. "Behave yourself."

His protests were met with a pointed stare. Fair. But he still didn't appreciate the implication.

A bell tinkled as the door shut behind them. The interior of the shop was warm and riotously colorful from the bolts of jewel-toned fabric hanging from racks about the room, every surface gilded in lantern light. The air smelled faintly of roses. Rugs and mats cushioned the clay-tiled floor. Fine gold chains hung like garlands between the lanterns, shivering and jingling like bells in the draft they had brought in with them. At this time of night, he had expected the place to be empty. It was anything but. Customers—none of them human—were scattered along the length of the long, narrow shop, sitting on the low couches, browsing bolts of fabric and trinkets. An entire section of the wall was dedicated to fanciful hats decked in pearl netting and various oddities. One hat looked as if it might hold a live bird. He hoped he was mistaken.

Belar hesitated. This had seemed like a much better plan out on the street. Now he wasn't so sure.

His unease only grew at the sight of one particular customer. Pointed ears, more sharply tipped than his own, hair the color of moonlight on the water. The Fae stood speaking to a young man wearing an apron, a worker probably, in the far corner of the room. Then their eyes picked out first Cassian and then Belar. He fought to stay still. As far as he knew—which was admittedly almost nothing where the Fae were concerned—there was no way to tell him from any other human unless he wished it. Or unless he did something silly like try to run away.

Cassian's hand on his arm tightened almost to the point of being painful.

"What is it?" Belar asked, grateful for the distraction.

"I see a familiar face." His jaw clenched.

Belar couldn't find whoever he meant and the more he looked around the harder it was to keep his eyes from straying back to the corner of the room. He'd only seen a Fae once before, as a child, and he felt a little of that same wonder now. *Notice me*, his traitorous heart whispered. The words felt tattooed on his body. A plea that terrified him with its urgency. He moved to put Cassian between them.

"This is a tailor," he pointed out. Unnecessarily, since Cassian was the one who had tricked him into coming here in the first place.

"Among other things, yes."

"I was expecting something seedier, not a respectable business. You could have prepared me." He fished out the small pouch of coins he'd liberated from unwary pockets the day before. They hadn't needed them as much as he had needed to not be completely without funds.

"Where did you get all that?" Cassian murmured.

Belar ignored him, dumping the lot into his palm and sorting them into little piles as he counted with increasing discomfort. "I can't afford any of this," he hissed. He didn't need to ask prices in this shop because clearly the cost was going to be *too much.* He'd had to save for months just to buy a second pair of boots earlier this year and this place reeked of extravagant spending.

"You don't have to. Consider it a perk. The trip will be useful in a number of areas." He took Belar's hand and turned it palm up so that he could press a kiss to the thin skin there. It was unfair how good that felt.

"Well, this *is* a surprise," said a voice from beside them. Belar snatched back his hand and hid it in a pocket. The memory of Cassian's warm lips still burned the center of his palm. "I didn't even know you were back."

Cassian straightened, smile already in place. "It was only a matter of time, Marisol."

So, this was Marisol—not that the name meant anything in particular to Belar, but he didn't need to know who she was to see she was stunning. Dressed in a long, belted tunic of burgundy and wide pants beneath, hair cropped close to the scalp, and ebony skin dusted with some kind of glittering powder. She smiled prettily, full lips parting to reveal the double set of fangs beneath. They were shorter and duller than the fangs of any vampire he had met so far, barely showing at all, which meant she probably wasn't one. She also lacked the amber eyes.

Marisol stepped closer and rested a hand on Cassian's arm before her attention turned to Belar. "And who is this? We haven't been introduced."

"He is the reason we're here," Cassian offered. "One of them anyway. Do you have anything to suit?"

Her eyes widened. "I think I just might. But a human? Really?" She ran an appraising eye over

Belar, and he noted the beginnings of a question in her expression. Then the look turned sly. She smiled. "Does Leya know about this?"

"No."

"Interesting." Marisol's smile widened. "I regret I won't be there to see the show. But let's get you fitted, hmm?" Belar was detached from Cassian's side despite his protests and handed off to an assistant. The girl ushered him toward a door on one wall. Her grip on his arm was surprisingly firm. The hallway beyond split into a string of smaller rooms. He heard the chatter of voices and the metallic churn of sewing machines behind their closed doors. Someone emerged from one of the rooms with arms weighed down with bolts of bronze and green fabric. He paused at the sight of Belar before bowing and heading in the opposite direction.

"Be gentle with him. He's a bit shy," Cassian said.

As he was dragged through the door and toward this strange and beautiful new torture, Belar swore the vampire would pay for this.

Chapter Eight

"Be gentle with him. He's a bit shy?" raged Belar, the violence in his voice somewhat hampered by the small stack of parcels in his arms as he stepped out of the shop and onto the street to rejoin Cassian. "What was that?"

"Highly entertaining, for one thing," Cassian said just for the enjoyment of watching the hunter's face turn red. He looked like he might throw something soon. "But also very informative. Thank you for being an excellent distraction. I don't think I've ever seen Marisol so happy. You wanted information and now we have it," he added in a lower voice. It wasn't wise to talk about these things out on the street, even here. Especially here. He relieved the hunter of the packages, took them back into the shop to be delivered to the house, and then gestured down the street. "Shall we go?"

"I don't know about you, but I intend to find food. Immediately. I doubt your cousins have anything I can eat and I'm about to faint dead away," Belar said. He looked up and down the darkened street, but at this time of night most everything was dark and closed up. While he considered, he tapped one foot against the damp cobbles.

"You want to eat? Again? You just ate the other day."

The hunter met his eyes. A lock of his dark hair had come loose from its tie and the breeze blew it into his face. He brushed it aside. "*Yes*, I want to eat *again*. It's been nearly two days since I had more than a few scraps—which I had to steal I might add. I submitted to your games with the tailor, I ache, and I'm hungry. So, help me find someplace in this city that is still open and serving food at this hour or so help me I will stab you."

Cassian stared.

Belar folded his arms over his chest and stared back with a defiant toss of his head. As an afterthought, he said, "Please. And while we're there you can tell me what you've learned."

It was the please that got Cassian. Such a small word to carry such vulnerability. "Would you really have stabbed me?"

"Without hesitation."

"Then I'd best do as you say."

He guided Belar on with a hand at the small of his back. Beneath his touch he could feel the shift of muscle and bone, the faint quiver of heartbeat and lungs—of life—but there was no sign of the hunter pulling away from him. If anything, he seemed to shift closer. The movement was so subtle he wasn't sure he hadn't imagined it. He glanced down, gauging the distance between them. Belar, still looking ahead, didn't even notice. "I think I may know a place. It isn't far."

*

Luckily the place Cassian had been thinking of still existed. It wasn't until they'd found a table and were soaking up the comforting warmth inside that he remembered it had been nearly eighty years since he'd been through the door. It could have burned down or been abandoned in that time. The idea filled him with a fresh wave of disorientation.

Everything appeared the same as it had when he went to ground, but it was only a thin covering, like cheap paint, that scratched away at the slightest scrape.

The tables were arranged in similar formations and the walls were still covered in framed art but where it had been landscapes and florals before now the walls were largely given over to large posters with colorful text outlined in black and people rendered in bold, almost ugly lines of paint. Rows of dancers and singers in tall, feathered hats stared out at him from the frames. Their expressions threatened attack. Even the diners around them were unfamiliar though some were kin. He might recognize *what* they were, but he had no idea *who* they were or where they'd come from. None of them seemed to know him either. He still remembered a time when just entering a room had pulled a veil of silence over a crowd. Granted, to him that time was mere months ago instead of decades and the silence had been one of fear, but the end result was the same: another reminder that everything else in the world had moved on and they had done it without him. Eventually it would stop hurting.

He settled into his chair, resigned to brood and be uncomfortable until it was time to leave again.

Somehow the hunter was already ordering. He slapped a fistful of coins down on the tabletop and aimed a hopeful look at the server. "What will this get me?"

As it happened, it would get him quite a lot.

Cassian eyed the coin purse as it disappeared into one of the hunter's pockets again. It was made of worn mauve silk, one side adorned with a beaded peacock. He would have noticed it. "Where did you say you got that? I don't remember seeing it among your things before."

"When you stripped me of my clothes while I was in a weakened condition?" Belar asked archly. His eyebrows rose behind the wire frames of his spectacles.

"Yes, exactly that. You make it sound quite filthy, but alas it was the maid who saw to you until you'd been patched up. I only saw the results. And the contents of your pockets. That purse wasn't among them."

Belar stared at him in unbroken silence until his meal—all three dishes of it—had been delivered to the table and they were as alone as they could be in a room full of assorted people and non-people. "Wine?" He presented the bottle for Cassian's inspection.

Cassian shook his head. “I don’t drink wine. But thank you.”

Belar filled his own glass almost to overflowing. He looked down, hands fluttering as he decided which dish to choose first, eventually settling on the bowl of some kind of spiced stew sprinkled with toasted pumpkin seeds which he popped in his mouth before he took up the spoon. He pointed it at Cassian. “If you must know, I picked a few pockets after I left your cousins’ house, but not from anyone who couldn’t spare it. They probably won’t even miss what I took. I do have *some* scruples.”

“And a very convenient way of exercising them.”

His tone earned another glare. It might have been more effective had the hunter stopped spooning stew into his mouth while he did it. The bowl was already half empty. A testament to how hungry he’d claimed to be.

Cassian eyed the other two dishes—one plate filled with some kind of sausages and wilted greens and the other a mound of hashed vegetables with an egg oozing over the top. “Are you sure this will be enough to satisfy you?”

He had no idea how much food was normal since it wasn’t something he needed himself. Blood was more than enough to sustain his kind. Some still ate a few nibbles here and there, to blend in and appear more human, out of curiosity, or what have you. He’d once attempted to eat an apple since humans claimed to enjoy them so much. It had gone rather poorly.

Belar paused, spoon to his mouth as he licked it clean with a dart of his pink tongue and met Cassian's eye. "What is it? Are you hungry? I can order more."

Cassian looked away. "No. I'm not."

"Just ornery then. I see." He traded the empty bowl for the plate topped with an egg and poked the yolk until it ran down over everything beneath. Made a contented little noise. "Is the sudden brooding to do with this current mess or whatever put you in the ground? You never did explain why you were sleeping, not fully. I admit I've become a little curious."

Cassian was inclined not to answer. His resolve lasted right up until the moment he glanced at the hunter again and saw the naked interest in his eyes. Something about it made him want to explain, to open like one of Arakiel's precious little night blooming flowers when looked at by the moon. Was it the fact the hunter was actually looking *at* him? Seeing him? How long had it been since that had happened? And how tragic was it that even this much attention felt like flattery to him? From a human to boot.

"You really wish to know?"

Belar leaned his elbows on the table, propping his chin on folded hands, and nodded. "I really do."

"Then how about we trade? A story for a story. I will tell you mine and you will tell me..." Cassian thought a moment. "Tell me why you became a hunter."

"No."

"Then you will have to resign yourself to ignorance. How unfortunate." He couldn't resist a little laugh at the hunter's expression.

Belar took a gulp of his wine. Grumbling. "Fine. Fine. But you have to go first."

"Of the two of us, which has already reneged on an oath? I can't quite recall."

"You're an ass."

"I've been called worse. But I never said I wouldn't explain either." Cassian met the hunter's eyes. Maybe once his curiosity had been sated his interest would wane and Cassian would be able to stop thinking about the curve of those lips and what it would feel like to trace them with his tongue, to have the hunter open to him in return. He'd spent hours tortured by the memory of the hunter on his knees already. He needed to stop. "You don't actually know what the Right Hand does, I assume?"

Belar shook his head.

"I figured as much from your initial reaction. As a whole, the kin are not especially organized. And it isn't necessary since there are so few of us these days and other than the general expectation that we mind our own business there isn't much to govern. But we do adore a good spectacle anyway. You've met Arakiel," he said with a wry smile. "So, a very long time ago the country was split up amongst the eldest and fiercest to protect those who choose to remain in what little society we have. I don't know how things are done elsewhere, but here this is the way. Each ruler—whether prince, princess, or prinx it makes no matter—has several others behind them. Advisers." A nod. "And one to protect their ruler and carry out their will. That was me."

Belar stilled. "You're saying you were—"

"An assassin of sorts, yes. Or bodyguard perhaps is more accurate. I killed what needed killing and coerced what didn't. And I served my princess faithfully for over a century. In every way." Cassian snickered at the slight hitch in Belar's breathing. The telltale widening of his eyes that predicted his moods. He probably didn't even realize he'd done it. "I came to her as a lover first, if that's what you're wondering. I was young and it was flattering to be coveted by someone so many others wanted. The rest came later, and I was happy enough to do it for her." He sighed. "Until I wasn't anymore. She didn't take my decision particularly well."

An understatement. They had barely even been lovers at that point, more a habit stretched thin and turned ugly; too much history between them to walk away and too much between them to stay. If there had been any way to fix it, to reset the past and fix *them,* he had never been able to divine it and being the Right Hand had left him too exhausted to try anyway.

Cassian spread his hands. "We fought. I won. And I left behind everything I'd been for one hundred and sixty"—he tipped back his head as he counted them off—"three years. I think. She might have exiled me, but I didn't stay around long enough for her to try. Instead I found myself a nice quiet patch of land where no one could find me and I went to sleep. Until you came along."

"It always comes back to that," Belar grumbled without meeting his eyes.

"That *is* why we're here. Though I find myself minding the circumstances less and less." He lowered his gaze, taking in the hunter's unfinished dishes and his hand resting lax and half curled on the table. Belar had removed his gloves to eat. Cassian couldn't remember if he'd seen them bare before. The knuckles were rough, old scars giving the skin an uneven texture, little finger crooked where it had broken and healed imperfectly. He wanted to follow the faint blue map of veins running along the back of that hand with his fingers. To keep tracing until he found his way back to the source.

Cassian had never been so close to a human for so long. At first he'd thought the impulse to touch and smell and *taste* was just a distorted sort of curiosity. Boredom assuaged by the arrival of a new plaything. But it wasn't. He wanted the hunter. In every sense that the word could be intended, he *wanted.*

He tore his eyes away from the hunter's hands.

"Now your turn," Cassian said.

Rather than answering, Belar stabbed a sausage from his plate and took a bite. Chewed, lips glistening with oil. He finished the rest of the plate and half his wine before he said a word.

"I don't have a sad story of vengeance if that's what you're expecting. My family wasn't killed by vampires. My mother is quite content, in fact. Or she was, last I saw her." He dabbed at his mouth with the napkin and then dropped it back into his lap. His lips puckered in a considering frown. "I was attacked. Late one night while returning from my lessons. I never even saw the creature. Something knocked me straight over, so hard I cracked my head against the cobblestones, and next thing I knew there were claws and I was bleeding. So much blood I could smell it. And taste it. I don't remember much else. Everything was wobbly from hitting my head and it was so dark I could barely even see, but a hunter heard me screaming. Saved my life." He shrugged, all nonchalance, but his eyes were far away. "When I healed enough to sneak out of the house again, I tracked her down and convinced her to take me on as a sort of apprentice. Took some doing. She didn't want to at first. Said it was too dangerous, it wasn't the usual way. I think most of them come to it through family. Or military. Those ones don't like me much." Cassian didn't miss the mischievous curve of his lips. Then the look bloomed into a real smile full of fondness. "But eventually I got my way and she agreed to train me. Ysa is retired a long time now, but I still see letters from her sometimes."

"How old were you?"

Belar blinked. "Oh. Um. Not very. Seventeen." He tipped more wine into his glass, spilling a little as his hand shook.

"And yet so motivated to leap into danger. Why?"

"I'm not going to answer that." Belar's eyes were wide again as he hid behind his wineglass, drinking so long and so deeply it seemed his intent was to drown himself at the bottom so he wouldn't be forced to speak again.

"A secret reason then. Something important to you."

The hunter's gaze followed him over the rim of his glass. He'd gone spectacularly red again. His heart beat so loud Cassian could scarcely hear anything but its heady drumming. It sounded like it was calling out to him.

"Finish your food."

Which he did, mopping up the remnants with scraps torn from a roll. He avoided looking up except when he thought Cassian might not be looking back.

"What information did my anguish buy you?" Belar asked after they'd been sitting in silence a while.

"Was it really as bad as all that?" The few times Cassian had caught sight of him, the hunter had been practically glowing.

"It was absolute torture." He sat up as he warmed to the topic. "I didn't even know half those fabrics existed before tonight and now I'll forever be tormented by the knowledge that I can't have them.

Silk and lace are hardly appropriate attire for trudging through cemeteries."

"I can think of a number of other activities that might be enhanced by them." He studied Belar's profile, the pouting turn of his lower lip, the high arch of his brows. Cassian could imagine quite a lot of reasons to wrap him in silk, delicate trails of lace, and even more reasons to unwrap him again.

Belar met his gaze. The way his tongue swiped over his lower lip was probably completely innocent, but Cassian couldn't help viewing it with different eyes. He wanted it to be an invitation.

"I'm sure you could. But the information?" Belar asked, a touch of humor coloring his tone. "You were saying?"

"Ah. Yes. That." He packed away his imaginings with some regret. "There have been a few absences of late. Normally it's not so surprising. Most of the kin scatter during the longer days of the year. Take refuge. Some cross over to get away from the threat of the sun." At Belar's look he clarified. "To the shadow realms, or the outer edge at least. *From the dark we came and to the dark we will return,*" he quoted. It was an old tale among the kin, but he doubted humans knew more than a scrap. The hunter and scholar in Belar would probably appreciate hearing the full telling someday, just as he seemed to enjoy all those storybooks he'd had back at his cottage. He folded his hands together. "But we can't survive there for long. No humans means no ready food and eventual starvation. It isn't pretty. But it's a pleasant enough place to visit. Near endless night. No humans hunting us. Some call it home."

"Sounds charming," Belar said dryly.

"There are aspects of it I think you might enjoy. But that isn't the point I'm trying to make. Locating anyone is a bit of a task at the best of times. We aren't known for our...cooperation. Outside of family connections it's safer to keep to ourselves. However, with the seasons turning and the nights getting longer most should have returned if they were planning to. The Long Night is only two months away and that inspires at least a weak sort of camaraderie. Most attend the festivities one way or another. Even Erathel and Arakiel take part. But according to Marisol two of her regular customers haven't resurfaced yet, young vampires. They were a couple, but I've been gone so long I'm not entirely sure they still are. She told me where I might find them if they stayed within the city. It could be nothing, but it is odd of them to disappear so suddenly."

"Maybe they're just late sleepers."

Cassian huffed a laugh. "It's possible. But Demetria placed a dress order months ago, paid for in advance, and she hasn't gone to collect it. That's unlike her."

"Where do they live? Or nest? Or whatever it is you call it."

"Live will suffice. And why?"

Belar grinned at him. It was the most beautifully wolfish expression he'd ever seen. "Because I think it's time I met some more vampires, don't you?" He pushed back from the table and stood.

And then almost crashed backward onto the floor. Would have if Cassian hadn't caught him.

"I might have drunk a bit too much," Belar said. "I'll be fine."

"We can track them down tomorrow. You can't go like this."

"I can."

"All right, you *can*. But I would prefer to refrain until you're able to stand on your own, for my own peace of mind. I don't know what kind of mood we'll find them in—if we find them at all. You might attack them and hit me instead."

He expected more of an argument, but Belar only nodded, still clutching at Cassian's arms to keep from tipping.

*

Belar stared up at the ceiling in the darkened bedroom. Something terribly close to despair coursed through him.

He had enjoyed dining with the vampire earlier. With Cassian. Not as enemies temporarily allied out of necessity and soon to betray each other but as...friends. Possibly something else besides. There had been several moments during the meal when Cassian's eyes had darkened and Belar had known what he was thinking as clearly as if it was written on the air between them. In those moments he'd wanted it too. Whatever was going on behind Cassian's eyes, he wanted it.

He'd even been strangely touched by Cassian's concern as he escorted Belar back to the house to sleep off his accidental drunkenness. This wasn't supposed to happen.

He was becoming fond. Fond of a vampire. Fond of a vampire he had attempted to kill twice already. That last detail was the least unusual thing about the situation as far as he could tell and the part he clung most tightly to.

What was he doing?

And further, what did he *want* to be doing?

He rolled over and buried his face in the pillow with a soft moan.

What he needed was sleep. Maybe that and sobriety would cure him of whatever fantasy had taken hold of him tonight and he would be able to stop imagining fangs at his neck and hands on his body. And when that was done, he could forget the idea that there might be anything else between them too.

Chapter Nine

The vampires, as it turned out, had helped themselves to an abandoned house in an outer ward of the city where they were unlikely to be disturbed. According to Cassian there were other vampires and dark things lurking in the shadows, earning the area a reputation for being haunted. Belar could see why as soon as they drew close.

The street was rutted with old wheel tracks and the buildings all had a slouching, sooty look as though they were only waiting for a convenient moment to give up the pretense of being inhabitable and tumble down around them. Lampposts rose out of the darkness like forgotten sentries. No lamplighter had visited them in a very long time.

Belar had no idea what the neighborhood had looked like a century ago, but in the present, it looked dreary. Even the ethereal blue glow of the moon couldn't make this place beautiful. It only made it appear lonelier.

"How miserable to live in a place like this," Belar muttered.

"I suppose it is. I wouldn't know." Cassian drew up next to him and folded his arms. "I spent much of my time elsewhere as I said. And now...I suppose I live with my cousins." He looked momentarily puzzled before he shrugged. "I may have to take up gardening. Arakiel will no doubt insist."

"Oh, the horror."

"It is a little. I don't think I'm fit for nurturing sprouts and making things grow."

"You prefer killing them, I suppose." Belar snickered quietly. It was a strange thing to joke about but he couldn't help himself.

"Not anymore, no." He paused, that vague expression still clouding his eyes. "Do you?"

"Do I what?"

"Prefer the killing."

He was tempted to give the flippant answer. It was another of the hunters' unspoken rules that they didn't discuss their reasons for doing what they did. It was messy work. Dangerous work. Sometimes morally questionable work. The less they dug into each other's affairs, the better. Everyone deserved a few secrets to bury undisturbed. And yet Cassian kept bumping up against the truth like it was an infected tooth he was obliged to extract. Belar didn't know how to lie in the face of such blatant curiosity, or not in the face of *his* blatant curiosity at any rate. He lied perfectly well all the rest of the time.

"It's necessary. Sometimes." He hoped that would be the end of it.

The vampire nodded. There was no way to tell if he meant it in agreement or only to show he'd heard.

Damn him. And damn himself because his mouth was already open, words tumbling into the space between them in a way he'd never intended but couldn't seem to stop. "I think about my students sometimes. Alone in the dark. Helpless. I would want someone to be there to protect them if they needed it. If I couldn't be—" He swallowed the sudden clot of feeling that stuck in his throat. "—I want to believe someone else would be. Ysa was there for me. And perhaps I'll be that hunter for someone else whether I know it or not." He clutched at his usual nonchalance and pulled it back around him. Forced his voice flat. "A regular circle of life."

"That's surprisingly noble of you."

Belar bristled. "Fuck you."

"I meant that honestly," Cassian said in a quiet voice.

"Oh."

"It's a respectable reason."

"I didn't ask for your approval."

"I know."

Belar frowned and shook his head. What had he done to deserve this? "Forget it. We're wasting time talking when I should be climbing in that window"—he pointed to one whose glass had already been broken out—"there."

"Or you could try the door."

"Amateurs go in doors," Belar said, mood improving by leaps and bounds at the prospect of breaking and entering. "Besides, the second floor is closer to the attic. More defensible position for hiding especially around here. The river is close, and this area is low lying enough to be prone to flooding. Cellars are probably useless if they exist at all. Though that's assuming these vampires of yours are in hiding. If they're dead, it won't matter which way we enter."

He didn't wait for any further comments before Belar started picking his way across the street and into the ruined lot around the house. It hadn't taken long to cross town, but it was hard to tell what time it was without a watch. No sense wasting whatever remained of the night. He wanted answers. Hopefully a few would be inside.

The window he'd chosen was only a short climb up, but before he could find his first handhold there was an arm around his waist, pulling him against a firm body. "Erathel will never let me hear the end of it if you ruin that outfit," Cassian murmured and then they were up. Belar had barely had time to brace hands against shoulders before they were in the upper room, the bare casement of the window behind them, and Cassian was stepping away again.

"Well, you certainly do have your uses," Belar said sweetly.

"Is that the only one you can think of?"

"For now." Their eyes met. There was something there again. Like a flash of lightning illuminating a whole landscape he'd never imagined before. It tugged at everything he had been working so hard to bury.

So last night wasn't just an anomaly after all.

Shit.

Belar turned on his heel, studying the room. It was in shambles. Broken furnishings sat in the darkened corners, forming a lumpy mountainous backdrop to the otherwise empty room. Exposure had weathered the floorboards in uneven streaks. He stepped lightly. It wouldn't have been unexpected to break through the floor. It had happened before in places twice as well kept as this one and he still had scars on his calf from the experience. "Charming," he muttered.

"It is indeed something of a downgrade from what I remember of them," Cassian said. Belar flinched at the reminder that he was still right behind him. He hadn't forgotten. That was impossible. But he had been trying extremely hard to focus elsewhere and now his effort was ruined. Cassian ran a hand along the warped door jamb as they stepped into the hallway as though he were searching for something.

"So you do know them."

"We weren't friends. It was my job to know everyone. And you might be surprised how easy that is when the faces stay the same century after century."

Each room they inspected was as empty as the last until finally Belar faced the narrow ladder to the attic. The trapdoor hung open in invitation, a scrap of bedraggled lace caught on a splinter dangling down like a pennant. He couldn't resist a triumphant smile in Cassian's direction. It was a mistake. Whatever indifference he'd once had to the vampire, it was gone now, and the wide curve of that mouth was starting to look all too agreeable. Despite the fangs? Or because of them? He didn't know anymore.

Instead of considering it, he climbed the ladder.

It was warmer above. He could feel it as his head came through the open trapdoor and he clambered over the edge. The attic space was large and open, the slanted beams supporting the roof giving it a cathedral-like illusion of height. Rugs covered the battered floor and a glowing lamp hung from the exposed beams above. It swayed in the draft that snuck through the cracks in the roof. A small sitting area had been arranged along one wall, partially curtained off with silk scarves hung over a laundry line.

An angry hiss alerted him to the fact the room wasn't as empty as it had initially appeared. Funny. He'd always thought the hissing was a myth too.

The vampire dropped on him, slamming Belar to the floor so fast it made his head spin. He was *really* getting tired of them doing that. Before they could try anything else, he planted a boot in their stomach and kicked them away, rolling sideways to avoid the swipe of claws. Then he was up again, knife in hand, to face them. Cassian had gotten there first. The new vampire struggled in his grasp, but he'd gotten them by the back of the neck and it was obviously a losing battle.

"Hello to you, too, Demetria," Cassian said.

"Let go. I said let go." She aimed a clawed hand at his face, but he just leaned out of the way, unbothered by how close she'd come to his eyes. All her struggling threatened to topple her upswept hair. Curly black tendrils were already unraveling around her face. "What are you doing here, you shit? This is private property. You're supposed to be dead to the world." Her dress looked ready to pop a seam as she reached behind her to dislodge his grip on her collar. It was at least three years out of date and the beading down the front of the bodice sagged where a thread had come loose. No wonder she'd ordered a new one.

"Yes, well, now I'm not. Believe me, I'm just as disappointed as you." Cassian set her down as gently as if he'd just discovered she was made of porcelain and stepped aside. "And you're not dead at all. We wondered."

"We? We who?" She scowled, the look twisting her otherwise smooth face into something which looked much older. It was funny how much vampires looked their age when they were displeased but rarely ever any other time. Her gaze fell on Belar. If possible, her sneer intensified. "Oh. You keep pets now." It wasn't a question.

Cassian put out a hand to hold Belar back. "He's not a pet." He swept the surprisingly cozy expanse of the attic with a searching glance. "And where is Adrien?"

She shook her head.

"Esther?"

Another shake.

"Kosta?" That got the reaction none of the other names had.

Demetria hissed, fangs standing out in a way that put Belar in mind of cats when they got their hackles up. "He and Meredith ran off together. Weeks ago. Stole everything we had, including my Adrien's heirlooms. Little shits. If you find her, you're welcome to do as you like. She deserves that kind of lesson." She stared at Belar the entire time she spoke. "It's rude to hold silver on your host, human. Put it away."

"Oh, is this a social call? I'm ever so sorry." But he sheathed the knife again. With Cassian blocking him he couldn't stab her anyway. Even though he was beginning to suspect she would deserve it if only for the way she was looking at him like he was a roast on a spit.

"Which heirlooms of Adrien's did they take?"

With another scowl she retreated to the side table. She pulled out a pack of clove cigarettes and lit one from the lamp before she turned back. "Not sure. There was a box. He wouldn't let anyone touch it, not even me, but I remember a ring. He wore it sometimes, just for a while, and then he would put it back and lock everything up again."

"A ring. With a blue stone? Gold filigree?"

Somehow Cassian's arm had found its way around Belar's waist again, each finger a small point of warmth and pressure even through the sleek fabric of his coat, and he didn't dare move and draw attention to it.

"That's the one." She puffed a cloud of smoke in their direction. She flounced into one of the chairs nearby, still smoking, still scowling, and crossed one leg over the other. She had no shoes on beneath her long skirts. One toe poked through her worn stockings. "He was in a state when he found out. Disappeared right after them looking fit to bleed anyone who got in the way so I figured that was it. You know how he gets. He's all sweetness until you set him off. But then he came back looking scared and beat half to shit." She looked between Cassian and Belar. "That's why you're here, isn't it?"

"It's possible," Cassian said.

She nodded slowly. "That's what I figured. He said when he found where they'd gone something had gotten there first, a shadow beast. Tore everything up, including Kosta. No sign of Meredith. Then it came after him. He only got away because of sunup, but it came back looking for him the next night." She stopped. Her eyes rested on Belar. "Do we know you?"

"I doubt it. What happened the next night?" he prompted. She'd stopped looking at him like a meal, but this new appraisal was almost worse. It made him feel as if his ears were showing.

"Funny thing. Adrien ran out to fight the thing off, thought he would be so noble about it and let me get to safety. I was watching from the window and the beast wasn't alone. There was a human with it, looked like they were...talking. Somehow. Didn't know the beasts could do that."

"A human? Not kin? You're sure?" Cassian asked. His fingers twitched against Belar's side.

"I'm sure."

"Could you see their face?"

She shook her head. "It was covered. Wasn't much to see besides the eyes."

"How long ago was this?"

Demetria shrugged. She tucked the cigarette between her lips and started repinning her hair, wrapping locks around the larger coil atop her head. "Couple weeks," she said at last. "Summer was already fading out, praise be. Why?"

Cassian nodded, that thoughtful hum rumbling deep in his throat. "No reason in particular."

The liar. She knew it, too, but said nothing, only puffed again on her cigarette until she was lost in a cloud of her own making.

"Where is Adrien now?"

"Somewhere you'll never find him." Her smile was all scorn. "Now you and your pet can see yourselves out. Forget we spoke. Adrien is done with all that mess. Leave him be. You can tell your princess that."

"She's not—" Cassian snapped before he caught himself.

"Mmhmm. You'll go back eventually. You always do." She waved them off and went to stand beside the single narrow window at the far end of the attic, but Belar noticed she didn't turn her back completely. Her eyes stayed trained on Cassian. He couldn't say he blamed her.

They left the way they came, though this time Cassian's grip was overly tight as he lifted Belar. Distracted.

"You really aren't over that princess of yours, are you?" Belar asked when he'd been set back down on the broken pavement of the yard.

"What?"

"I can't think of any other reason why she wouldn't be your first suspect in this. You said things ended badly and you fought. Did you even consider that she might be the one before you started looking elsewhere for someone to blame?" He had to pick up his pace to match the vampire's stride. It was getting longer by the second. If he kept this up, soon he would be flying over the pavement.

"Oh, I did. Believe me." His voice was dark as murder.

"And?"

"And I quickly came to the conclusion that if Leya wanted me dead there were easier ways. Even if there weren't, that still leaves the others unexplained. Killing a large portion of her former cabinet only lays suspicion at her door. That's unwise, especially in her position. The only law most kin adhere to is that we don't kill our own. Or if you do, you do it where no one can see you. She was never one to be sloppy about murder."

Belar almost tripped over his own feet. "Her cabinet? When were you going to share that last tidbit with me?" he demanded.

"I only just realized. It was the ring. We didn't all serve at the same time or in the same capacity, but we *were* together for one thing before we went our separate ways, a trial. The rings were her gift after—a thanks for our support—and Adrien completes the set. If he's hidden himself away as well as Demetria claims he might even survive until we've stopped all this. Lucky him."

"What were the rings a gift for?"

Whatever the expression on his face, Belar couldn't decipher it.

"What is—"

He didn't get to finish the question before the stink of decay reached his nose. He knew that smell just like he knew the unpleasant tingle in the air that followed. Cassian caught his arm and yanked him sideways. Belar yelped as he hit the wall. Cassian's body covered him. A spear of shadow shot through the space where he'd stood a moment before. The healing wound on his shoulder throbbed. As though being close to its source had awoken it. Too bad he didn't have a flare this time.

"Shit."

They ran, Cassian's grip on his arm threatening to pull him off balance. He had slowed to accommodate Belar, but he was still so much faster.

"I think someone is unhappy we're investigating," Belar said. He felt breathless. Not with fear but with excitement. At the chase. At making progress. The speeding tempo of his heartbeat in his ears made him feel whole. Right.

Then he looked back. That took a little of the edge off his mood.

The first shadow beast had been monstrous, malevolent and single minded despite the disturbing awareness lurking in its eyes. What pursued them now was solid shadow without face or any other discernible feature besides rippling darkness and the stink of decay, but he could still feel it watching them. That was worse. He never would have guessed that being stalked by an endless void would be so horrifying.

"Isn't this a bit excessive? What did you *do* to anger them?" Belar asked.

"I'm touched that you think it was all my doing. You make me sound like a first-rate villain. Unfortunately, I think you're as much to blame as I am this time. Is it still following?"

Belar couldn't turn again to look, not without falling. He didn't need to. They had taken several turns into the narrower back lanes and away from the main street, but the telltale darkness had kept pace with them. It crept further and further into his peripheral vision. He had the distinct impression of a great mouth about to close around him and he didn't like it. He didn't like it at all. He was one ill-timed stumble away from being eaten like a grape. "Yes. What is it? Professional curiosity," he panted.

"That?" Cassian glanced back as though he didn't already know. "*That* is just a shadow. What concerns me is what's on the other side of it. Don't let it touch you."

"Believe me, I hadn't planned on it." He reached for his knife, but Cassian stilled his hand.

"Save it. You can't fight the dark. Though I would dearly love to see you try."

A spidery hand shot out of the nearest patch of shadow toward his arm. Belar slashed at it with his knife. The thing let out a high metallic shriek. Apparently, it didn't need a mouth to scream. But the hand fell away. Where it had been, black fog hovered like mist before it, too, faded away. "You were saying?"

"I stand corrected."

Belar smirked.

Another whip of shadow streaked at them from the other side and Cassian swore. "Hang on."

His hands came around Belar, turning him so easily he didn't have time to react before he was hoisted half over Cassian's shoulder, an arm clamped tight against his hips so he couldn't wriggle free as he was carried.

The view was even worse when seen over Cassian's shoulder. The black wave was clearer now, half translucent like a throng of pursuing ghosts. As it moved, he could almost make out limbs, the suggestion of mouths, the hollow of eyes, but they were too numerous, the limbs too long. Its movements were the sinuous insectile slither of a centipede. Silent save for an eerie hum like voices whispering just beyond hearing. Everything about the creature was wrong. The shadow surged forward and before he could react it had grabbed a handful of Belar's coattails. He stabbed his knife at it but not before the fabric came away, leaving a ragged edge. The shadow had swallowed it.

"What *is* that?" he cried again. Because he had to say something. He'd seen plenty of monstrous beasts in his years as a hunter, but nothing like this. Nothing so completely unearthly. His free hand knotted in the shoulder of Cassian's coat.

"Don't let go."

For once, Belar did as he was told. There was a jarring lurch as Cassian jumped and another as they hit the side of a building and his fingers caught on the brick. One leap of Cassian's powerful legs had taken them up twenty feet like it was nothing. Gravity tugged Belar down. He clung to Cassian. This wasn't at all like climbing on his own. This was helplessness and adrenaline all wrapped up together, singing through his blood until he felt lightheaded. He was flying.

The ground receded. Cassian grunted. Stone scraped as he climbed higher and the patch of shadow fell away below, distance robbing it of some of its menace. Long dark arms dragged it up the brick after them, but Cassian was faster, leaping to a new building and then another, leaving it farther and farther behind.

Belar shifted to say as much to him and almost forgot everything, the drop, the shadow, everything but how black Cassian's eyes had become and the black claws tipping his fingers as he drove them into the brick and climbed higher. His dark hair fluttered in the wind.

"Stars preserve," Belar whispered through numb lips. Then he wrapped his arms tighter around Cassian's neck. Given the option of a fall into certain death and the arms of an uncertain one, he preferred the latter.

Cassian chuckled, the sound torn away by the wind as he leaped again.

*

They crashed down onto the balcony of the house, falling in the double doors and across the tile floor of one of the bedrooms like a wave. Belar sprawled on his back. Cassian spilled over him, still black eyed and vicious and beautiful, breathing hard from exertion. Belar's breath came in matching gasps. His heart thundered in his ears as Cassian raised himself, hands braced on either side of Belar's shoulders, claws grating against the tile. Barely inches from his neck. Their legs were still tangled together, Belar's body half pinned beneath the vampire's. A week ago, that would have worried him. A week ago, he would have called this a lie. Now all he could think of was what it would be like to kiss Cassian right now, whether his fangs would draw blood, whether he would even mind if they did. That might almost make it better.

Cassian ran one claw-tipped finger along Belar's cheek. His eyes fluttered closed at the touch, at the danger so close yet contained. Belar's hands fisted against the tile. The touch was repeated, this time grazing his lower lip. Gentle. So gentle. If the claws still remained, he couldn't feel them as he arched up into it. He wanted more. He wanted that hand around his throat. Holding him down. He ached for it. Like he'd been waiting years for this instead of days. Maybe he had been.

A small part of his mind told him no, but it was rapidly shrinking. It wasn't the voice of reason. It was the voice of caution and he had never been very good at that.

"We make a good pair, you and me," Cassian whispered like he was speaking directly into Belar's heart. Those quiet words spread through his veins like fire.

Belar opened his eyes. The blackness had faded from Cassian's eyes and the wind had left his hair tousled and wild as ruffled feathers. He could imagine his hands in it. He wanted to do more than imagine it.

"Do we?" Belar's voice was a rasp. He swallowed hard and Cassian's eyes followed the movement before his fingers traced the same path, one long drag from the underside of Belar's chin down the sensitive column of his throat that seemed to take forever. Belar was trembling by the time he reached the dip at the bottom.

"I think so."

Belar bit his lip. Cassian's eyes were on his, amber again, and so bright he couldn't look away. "Me too."

Then he pulled the vampire's mouth down to his.

Cassian's body covered his as Belar wrapped an arm around his neck, fingers slipping up to tangle in the vampire's hair like he'd been imagining. It was still cold from outside. Everything about him was cold except his mouth. Chilled fingertips brushed his neck, his jaw, tipping his head up as Cassian's lips moved against his and the dart of a hot tongue filled his mouth. Cassian tasted like fire and blood and Belar couldn't get enough of it. Whatever happened later, he wanted this now. Belar moaned. Cassian pressed a kiss to his jaw. Then his hand came up, angling Belar's head to the side before his mouth settled hot on his throat again.

"Are you afraid of me?"

Belar shivered as lips and teeth grazed his neck. "Do you want me to be?" His hands clenched on Cassian's shoulder and in his hair. Then they were carefully plucked away and pressed against the floor at either side of his head.

"Only a little." Cassian's eyes crinkled in amusement.

Belar leaned up in answer, trying to reach the mouth that was just out of his reach. He felt drunk in the best way. Cassian laughed. Then he leaned down again and brushed a kiss over Belar's parted lips. "I've been thinking about having you this way ever since I found you. Just like this. At my mercy." The last came as a low growl in Belar's ear before he pulled the lobe into his mouth, sucking. Pleasure lanced straight through him. Belar writhed helplessly, straining against the hands holding him down. Lost. He blinked hazy eyes. Moaned as Cassian kissed him again, slower this time. Oh, yes. He'd been waiting so long to feel something like this. Just like this.

Gradually the grip on his wrists loosened and Belar twined their fingers together instead. He didn't want to let go. Not yet. And Cassian lowered his head to nuzzle at his neck. "I thought it would be wonderful, but I had no idea how much. We should do that again," he said, words muffled against Belar's collar bone. "But later. Erathel is coming up the stairs." He lifted his head just high enough to catch Belar's eye, a question there. Waiting for Belar to pull away.

He stayed where he was. If he'd planned to feel ashamed of what they'd done, he wouldn't have done it in the first place.

Erathel announced herself with a smart rap against the door before pushing it open without waiting to be invited. Belar turned his head to look at her, his glasses going askew as they caught on his hair. It had fallen from its tie somewhere along the line and now Cassian was toying with it, wrapping strands around his fingers and gently tugging in a way that set off a riot of tingles across his scalp. If it was possible to melt more deeply into the floor, that would have done it. No one had ever done that for him before either. It was a sensation he could gladly become accustomed to.

She raised a single elegant eyebrow at the way they were tangled on the floor before turning to regard the open door to the balcony. "I see you've been busy. There's a shadow prowling the street outside."

Belar stiffened but there wasn't anything he could do with Cassian lying half over him and showing no signs of moving. "I'll handle it," Cassian said. Still without moving.

"It can't get in, can it?" Belar asked. Cassian had said something before, about protections on the house and his cousins themselves, but it was difficult to remember the details. He hadn't expected it to be important at the time.

Erathel didn't snort but it was heavily implied. "You'd best decide what to do about it soon. I already had to stop Arakiel going out to kill it once."

Cassian laughed, finally rolling over and standing up. He held out a hand to help Belar to his feet. "Bored with his plants so soon?"

"More like worried his little hedge witch won't visit with a monster on the doorstep. I would have been more concerned for the neighbors noticing, but then I realized I don't care." She paused to inspect her nails. "Come downstairs. You can explain what it is you've been doing over...a meal. Your human requires food, doesn't he?"

When she had gone out again and was less likely to overhear, Belar muttered, "I'm not a lapdog." He might be annoyed, but he'd come this far without dying and he intended to continue.

"They're not used to humans, or guests for that matter, but they are trying." At Belar's scowl he added, "I know that's not much of an excuse."

One thing had been bothering Belar as long as he'd been trapped in this house with them. "How *old* are they anyway?" Even compared to the other vampires he had met, there was something very different about them. Not just the blackness in their eyes. Something else beyond that. It was a feeling.

"Very old. Let's just leave it at that." When Belar started toward the door, Cassian caught his arm. "Wait. We were interrupted before I could finish explaining, but I've been considering."

For some reason those words filled Belar with dread. He didn't even know what he expected the rest of the statement to consist of but it took everything in him not to pull away. If they could just go back to the kissing everything would be so much simpler. "What is it?"

"I have an idea who might be on the other end of that shadow's leash."

Oh, thank the stars. Motives for murder were easier than sorting out his feelings.

Cassian shot him a curious look. "What did you think I was going to say just now?"

Belar couldn't answer what he didn't know himself, so he ignored the question. "Are you planning to tell me who has been attacking us or was I supposed to guess?"

Cassian raised the hand he still held to his lips and pressed a kiss into the palm. He aimed a crooked smile up at Belar. The sharp point of a fang grazed the sensitive flesh. Belar could feel it all the way down his spine. "I wasn't done with you yet, truth be told. Though Erathel is correct. We should handle the shadow before Arakiel gets to it." Then he tugged Belar against him.

"Why Arakiel?" Belar asked, breath catching as Cassian's hands smoothed down his back. It was still strange to realize he was enjoying every touch, that he still wanted more. He couldn't remember the last time he'd wanted someone this much, this quickly.

"Let us just say gardening isn't the only thing he enjoys." He gazed down at Belar before finally stepping away. "Anyway, do you recall that book I found in your library? The one belonging to Dismas?"

"It wasn't my library. It's communal. But yes. What of it?"

"Who retrieved that book?"

All the feeling drained from Belar's body and left him as cold as winter. "I did. Why?"

Cassian nodded. "It occurred to me that anyone who wanted revenge on me had waited a very long time to take it. I've been asleep for decades. So why now? And why act through intermediaries at all if one didn't have to? Any kin who has so many shadow beasts in their thrall is obviously old enough or powerful enough not to worry about retribution."

"Like your cousins," Belar guessed. He hadn't realized how different they were until tonight, seeing the others hiding in the dark, in torn-out buildings, like scavengers and thieves.

"Yes, like them. There's no reason someone like that would have to hire others to do their work for them. It's so much simpler, cleaner, to bloody one's own hands. More satisfying." His teeth flashed in a wolfish smile. Clearly, he knew what he was talking about. "Unless there was an additional reason that would make them unable. Say perhaps, being caught elsewhere."

Belar gave an uncomprehending shake of his head.

"Dismas had a... I'm not sure you could call her a parent, but she's as close to a mother as anything we kin have. She took him as her own as Erathel and Arakiel took me as theirs."

"Took you?" Belar frowned, mind already filling with snatched babies and blood.

Cassian looked amused. "The only families we have are those we make for ourselves. For protection. A new vampire is no better than a child for all that we're born full grown. I don't know what your myths say, but they're probably wrong. I look the same now as I did when my cousins found me. I've heard that some have memories of something before, but I didn't."

"That sounds lonely."

"I know no other way to be." Cassian shrugged. "But I was speaking of Dismas's mother. I haven't met her myself, but I know of her. She's very old. Very powerful. And she went to ground—a century ago at least. If she's woken again, it wouldn't surprise me at all to find she was behind this. It would also explain why you were chosen as...executioner. It's the sort of thing that one might find poetic."

"Well, I *don't* find it poetic. At all. And I think I could have lived without knowing an ancient vampire is angry with me. What are we going to do?" He had the few weapons he'd collected from headquarters and could acquire a few more if they could evade the shadow long enough to return there, but he still felt hopelessly unprepared for what was surely going to be a battle. Even the word battle felt enormous. Like it could swallow him whole. He pushed the feeling aside, mind already working toward a solution.

"We'll think of something. Together. Nothing can get in here without making a lot of noise first so we have a bit of time. But Erathel said something about a meal. You need to eat, yes?"

The idea of a vampire family dinner was almost more terrifying than the looming fight, but he took Cassian's hand when he offered it and followed him out of the room.

Chapter Ten

Belar followed Cassian down the stairs and to a warmly lit dining room paneled in dark wood. He hadn't seen this room yet, but it was every bit as extravagant and odd as the rest of the house. Everywhere he looked was a dream-like tableau. The room had no windows but where they might have been hung plates of obsidian and gold polished so smooth his distorted reflection stared back at him as he passed. The mahogany table had chairs enough for a dozen, the expanse lined with serving dishes on gold chargers and spiked gold candelabras wrapped in roses from the night garden. Not pink this time, they were so darkly red they were nearly black. Cassian's cousins completed the otherworldly image.

Erathel had taken the seat at the head with Arakiel on her left. They were both in burgundy tonight, Erathel's dress high-collared silk with wide velvet ribbons wrapping the bodice and Arakiel in a sheer gauze tunic open in a deep vee down to where it met the black silk sash. Belar could just make out the faint line of old scars on his chest, one on either side. At Cassian and Belar's entrance both of the vampires turned to watch them with black and gold eyes.

"Sit. We've been awaiting you," Erathel said as though they were urchins in a fairy tale just wandered in out of the wilderness. She gave no indication that she even remembered speaking to them upstairs.

Arakiel waggled beringed fingers and smiled. Belar assumed it was meant to be a friendly gesture but there were still too many teeth in that smile for his comfort.

Cassian took the seat at her right and helped Belar into the chair beside his. Place settings had been laid at every seat along the table and he had to wonder if they were expecting more guests or hadn't known they only needed four plates. So far, their knowledge of human manners was spotty at best, which probably accounted for the scraps of red lace laid over the plates in lieu of napkins. Belar took his and spread it over his lap anyway. It seemed rude not to. When Arakiel saw, he mimicked the gesture, smiling even more brightly.

At a nod from Erathel a silent complement of servants emerged from the shadows to remove the domed covers on the dishes and wield their arsenal of serving tools before fading away again. Belar's plate was piled with braised beef, tiny pearl onions, and a few other things he couldn't identify. One looked like a kind of almond pastry, out of place among the other savory foods cluttering his plate. Belar nudged it to the side so it wouldn't catch too much of the gravy. He was hungry enough that he would eat anything as long as it wasn't poisoned. He snuck a glance at Cassian. His plate bore half as much food and he was already poking at it with a butter knife and a look of curiosity. His brow furrowed as an onion rolled away from his attempts to stab it.

Erathel raised her wineglass in a silent toast before downing the contents in one long swallow. She held it out for a servant to refill. The carafe was of heavy dark glass so that the contents were shadowed, but whatever it held, it wasn't wine. Wine didn't coat crystal that way. He sincerely hoped they were as ethical about their blood consumption as Cassian claimed to be. "I trust some of this will suit. Forgive us for our lapse in hospitality yesternight. We meet so few humans." Her voice was low and musical and Belar still couldn't tell if she was amused or barely tolerating him. Her expression was as bland as ever.

"Thank you." He took a hesitant sip of the spiced wine in his own glass before he picked up his fork. How bad could it be, really?

As it turned out, everything was not just edible but...delicious. Even the strangeness of dining with three vampires couldn't keep him from devouring everything that touched his plate. It seemed as though they had arranged all this for his benefit so it would have been rude not to.

Every time he glanced at Erathel her plate looked the same until suddenly it was empty of everything but the remnants of the savory sauce. Across the table, Arakiel nibbled at small morsels with his fingers, but he seemed to time it to when Belar was watching him, finishing the move by licking his fingers clean with a languid sweep of his tongue. It was like dining with a pair of cats. He couldn't tell if they were playing with him or not. Cassian ate only a few bites from his own plate before pushing the rest away and folding his arms over his chest.

"You can stop pretending innocence," Cassian said. He watched Erathel as she took another measured sip from her glass. That was definitely blood. It stained her lips a berry red before she licked it away. "What do you know about Dismas's mother? Is she really awake?"

Erathel tipped her head. She stroked one hand down the long braid falling over her shoulder, smoothing it. "Is that what all this fuss has been about? I had no idea."

"Didn't you? I saw one of your spies. Following us in the market."

Belar stiffened. So that's who Cassian had spotted. It seemed so logical now.

"I told you he was too old for these games," Arakiel said, "but you never listen to me." He shifted in his chair, shaking back a long sleeve edged in gold beading as he raised his glass to be refilled. He saluted Cassian with it. "Bravo, lovely. And you, too, little hunter," he added with a grin at Belar. "I assume part of this revelation was your doing."

Erathel shot her brother an arch look which he ignored. "I promised not to interfere again, and I shan't. Though I could have," she murmured darkly. "But since you've asked, yes, I believe Scylla rose recently and has been regathering her strength somewhere nearby."

Belar's eyes narrowed. "Do you know where?"

Being under Erathel's scrutiny was like standing with his face in a bonfire. He was only waiting for his hair to catch fire. "I do not." The unspoken implication was that Scylla would no longer be anywhere if Erathel had known where to find her. Belar had to wonder if they had some personal animosity or if it was only a matter of Erathel not liking anyone else touching her things. And Cassian definitely qualified as one of her things. That probably didn't bode well for Belar either. His meal sat like a rock in his stomach.

"What about that shadow outside?" Belar said in an effort to turn the subject somewhere more useful, pressing a hand against his stomach to still the churning there. "If you don't know where this Scylla is, there must be another way to track her. Cassian said something was on the other end of that shadow. So how does it work? Like a door? Where does it lead?"

Erathel stared at him.

Cassian made a thoughtful face, thumb pressed against his lips. Lips Belar had just been kissing. Practically devouring. The strange turn of events made it seem almost surreal. Like it was something he had read about instead of something he had lived.

It was Arakiel who spoke first. “Oh, that’s clever. You want to use her own shadow against her.” Everyone turned to him as Arakiel beamed. His fangs were stained the faintest pink from the blood he’d been sipping while he watched them talk. “I’m glad I didn’t destroy it now.”

Cassian’s eyes glittered gold as he turned to look at Belar and took both his hands in his. His smile was so brilliant Belar couldn’t help but return it. “It may not be exactly like a door, but we can fix that. And then it will take us right to her.”

“Do we *want* to go right to her?” Belar had to fight not to look at Erathel and Arakiel. If this Scylla was half as old as they were, he didn’t relish the idea of facing her practically unarmed. But armed, that was a different story entirely. “Not that I’m against killing her. You hired me for an assassination, and I intend to deliver. But first I’ll need something to kill her *with*.” He bit at his knuckle as he considered. “I wish I had my axe. Though a flare would be a good start.”

He paused, belatedly remembering Erathel and Arakiel across the table. He lifted his eyes.

Arakiel laughed. “Oh, we already know exactly who you are, don’t worry.” He leaned forward over the table and his voice dropped to a conspiratorial whisper. His eyes captured Belar’s. The amber rings of his irises were nearly swallowed up by the black. “And I’m sure you know you can’t kill us.”

Belar nodded.

"Good." He beamed and sat back. "I think we'll enjoy having you around. Do your best not to die too quickly, hmm?"

Erathel raised a hand to signal one of the servants. "What is it you'll need?"

*

Cassian caught Belar by the arm as he paced past on the library rug for the third time. Holding onto him was like taking a bolt of lightning in his hands.

Belar had wound his long hair up into a tight twist at the back of his head and pinned it so it would stay out of the way. It made him look strangely gaunt. Frail even, with his long neck exposed and the faint trembling of the arteries visible beneath the skin. It made Cassian want to kiss him again. Once hadn't been nearly enough. Kissing Belar was an art he wanted to work at. To perfect.

But after the fire of the moment earlier something had slipped into Belar's expression whenever Cassian touched him. It was there now.

Cassian let his hand drop and Belar started away again. He made another half dozen loops before he came back to rest at Cassian's side. His lower lip was bitten almost bloody. Cassian resisted the urge to lick it clean.

Instead he asked, "What is it?"

Belar shook his head and then laughed, a quiet little puff of air that brushed Cassian's cheek. "I'm not used to operating like this, going straight at the things that want to kill me. I'm more comfortable with the element of surprise."

"Yes. I have noticed."

The brush of his fingertips on Cassian's neck just above his collar felt like a seduction. There was a small scar there from where the axe had rested. The edge was so keen it had parted flesh with only that gentle pressure before Cassian had woken to stop it from finishing the job. "And this is not the end I was expecting for this situation either." Belar's eyes met Cassian's, dark and unreadable, before he stepped back. "How much sunlight can you stand? What intensity? And how do you do it?"

Cassian blinked at the sudden change of topic. "What?"

"Sunlight. I know what I saw, and I need to know how it works. I've seen vampires in the sun." He hesitated, eyes darting away again, and Cassian could guess what it was he was thinking. Of other kin he had put to the sun. Cassian could so easily have been numbered among them. He'd stopped being angry about that so long ago. "They wither. They scorch. Your cousins are so old and even they hide from it. But not you. Why?"

Even a lengthy stare couldn't compel him to explain more so Cassian sighed. Then he began to unbutton his coat. Belar's face was almost reward enough, transforming his expression from guilt to a level of shock bordering on terror. A touch of anticipation as well. Cassian relished it. It was so difficult to surprise the man when he pulled out new tricks as easily as breathing, but this had finally come close. Cassian dropped the coat to the floor in a pool of expensive fabric. Arakiel would be horrified, but he would understand the need for a little drama. Pulling his tunic over his head so he stood bared to the waist wasn't strictly necessary either but oh, the way Belar's eyes followed was more than worth it too. Belar's mouth had fallen open the slightest bit and there was a cunning in his eyes that Cassian had only seen before when they fought. He liked it better now. Because this look had nothing to do with danger and everything to do with desire. It was possible they were one and the same with the hunter. Cassian had no complaint with that.

Belar cleared his throat, blushing as he looked away. "Was that necessary?"

"It was very necessary from where I'm standing. But for another reason beyond that." He tapped a finger against the large sigil tattooed on his abdomen just above the right hip. He knew it didn't look like much despite its size. A trio of upright lines, the middle longer than the others, overwritten by a circular band of characters so old there were only a handful left who could read them. Cassian wasn't among them. He had no interest in whatever it said, only in what it did.

"What is that? It looks like—" Belar leaned forward, absently adjusting his spectacles before he tipped his head down to look over the top of them anyway. One of his hands settled against Cassian's hip. The touch was perfunctory, but Cassian still imagined wrapping that hand with his own and bringing it to his mouth. Belar looked up at him with bright, distracting eyes. "Where did you get this mark?"

Cassian stepped out of his grasp. Maybe his teasing game hadn't been a brilliant idea after all. He hadn't considered the questions that would come after. They made it so much less entertaining. "Does it matter?"

"It might if that sigil is what I think it is. I've read about these from some of the old journals we've uncovered. But only descriptions; no one had a usable diagram or even a particularly *good* description. All hearsay. They were"—he waved a hand distractedly—"a sort of magical fairy tale, I thought. Granting power with a few lines and squiggles."

"And a great deal of pain," Cassian said, reaching for his tunic to put it back on. "Mustn't understate that part. But it's quite real." It hadn't felt like a fairy tale at the time. It had felt like being burned alive, but instead of ending in him a wisp of fading smoke it had gone on and on until he was sure nothing could be worth that amount of pain. He still rather felt that way. But it was impossible to deny the fact that the sigil had come in handy multiple times already. Twice just from his acquaintance with Belar alone.

"Pain?"

"Yes. Pain. I don't recommend it." The tunic slipped over his head, obscuring his vision for a moment, but Belar was still watching him with narrowed eyes when he'd finished. Cassian's glared back at him. "It's a very long story. I was...volunteered for the honor of being the first to test it. Years ago now." He laced his shirt back up to give his hands something to do. It really took a very long time to get the ends an even length. "If it worked successfully on me, others would follow. Right into the light."

Understanding traveled through Belar like a current. His mouth opened, but no words came out for a long time. Cassian waited, curious which of his questions would finally win out. "But if it worked, why didn't they...? Or did they?"

"It did work. You've seen the results with your own eyes. And before you ask, it isn't flawless. The sun still burns but in a controlled way. Leaves me tired. And full sun is like shards of glass in my eyes. My eyes weren't made for so much light. I won't die of any of it as far as I can tell. The ritual was a success, but I'm the only one who will ever use this sigil again. Don't worry."

"How do you know?"

"What an absolute tragedy it all was. Everything went up in flames soon after. Horrible," Erathel said, appearing just inside the library door as though she'd always been there. Cassian suspected she had been eavesdropping as usual. Waiting for a suitable moment to announce herself. Behind her hovered a knot of servants laden with supplies. "We shouldn't even speak of it." She pressed a hand over her heart and almost managed to look regretful. It was an impressive performance. "I believe we've found everything you asked for."

As she spoke, the items were arranged on the library table in neat rows. Knives. An axe. Though where they had found a silver one, and how they had gotten it here so quickly, was a mystery. A basket full of herbs and other ingredients. She stood by as they set everything out. Her hands hovered over the axe and other weapons before she dragged one finger down the silver blade. Cassian couldn't see her hand when she pulled away to know if it had burned her or how badly. "Will this do?"

"Perfectly. Thank you." Belar swept over, in his element again, murmuring his thanks even as he began sorting through everything they had brought him. He set out the mortar and threw pinches from different jars and packets into it, grinding everything together with even strokes.

Erathel nodded back and withdrew again but not before her eyes met Cassian's. She nodded once. It was as much of a blessing as she knew how to give.

"What is that you're doing there?" Cassian asked, turning away from the empty doorway and back to Belar. He was humming now. It shouldn't have been as charming as it was given the circumstances.

He frowned, working more urgently over the mortar. "It's a last resort if you care to call it that. I had hesitated to make it for fear of injuring you, too, but it seems that won't be a problem."

"More of that bottled sun of yours," Cassian guessed.

He got a tight nod in response.

"Suit yourself. Though I'm not sure what use it will be since we shan't give Scylla the chance to do anything but die swiftly. Safer that way."

Belar didn't look up. His hair was already slithering loose from its twist, drifting around his head in wavy tendrils. Cassian tucked a lock back behind Belar's ear. "Yes, we will. I plan to speak to her first. Alone if necessary. You hired me to remove a threat and I intend to deliver on that promise, but not until after I've said my piece."

"Scylla means to kill you—*us*. She's already tried at least twice now. And you want to chat with her instead of pressing our advantage while we can?" It was so ridiculous it seemed almost to make sense. For him at least. "What could you possibly have to say to her?"

"I knew."

The pestle scraped, stone against stone. Belar's scowl deepened. He sprinkled more of some herb they had clipped from the night garden. Cassian didn't know what it was or what it was called, only that it smelled sharp and green.

"With the vampire after you. I wasn't sure, not completely, but I suspected it wasn't right. Had a feeling. There was something different about the whole thing, too quiet, too peaceful. No bodies. Blue curtains in the window. It felt wrong." He drove the pestle down so hard that a pinch of his herbs puffed back out again and scattered over the table. "I killed him anyway. And ever since I've wondered how many others I've hunted might have been innocent, still vampires or what have you, but innocent enough. How many others did I kill for no reason? Or perhaps the wrong reason? So I'll talk to her first. Just to be sure. I need to."

*

Belar hadn't planned to say all that, but one word found its way onto his tongue, and then it had pulled all the others out with it, strung together like a strand of terrible pearls. They left a hollow in his chest where they had previously resided. An ache. If he listened hard maybe he could even hear the wind whistling through him. He had never liked the truth, and yet somehow, he couldn't stop speaking it around Cassian. Something in the vampire called to all the parts of Belar's heart that he had chained up in solitude and secrecy and he wanted so badly to do anything besides continue telling the truth. Who knew what other murky secrets it might bring to light? He had never had this problem before.

Tension thrummed in his muscles, digging fingers deep into his joints. He was wound so tightly now he would move like a toy soldier. A steady one-two beat. Marching time.

And it didn't make sense, what he'd said about talking to Scylla. He didn't need to look at Cassian's face and read whatever might lie in his expression to know that to the casual—and not so casual—observer it made no sense.

A plan to march in on a vampire, an elder vampire, who had been trying to kill them for days and...*talk*...

It wasn't a good plan.

It was the sort of plan one came up with when one intended to die, and he had no intention of dying which made his plan even more of a failure. It was a failure at failing.

Belar poured the herbs he had been abusing onto a waiting square of paper and refilled the mortar to begin again.

"Say something," he commanded.

"What is it you would like me to say?" The words were spoken in a tone of only idle curiosity.

He didn't know. He had been braced for mockery or disapproval. Disbelief. Possibly anger. He *was* after all in the business of killing vampires and had no plans of stopping despite his failure of a plan. He was the least likely candidate to earn sympathy with his sudden case of guilt.

Cassian leaned against the table beside him, his hip nudging it just enough that the mortar almost tipped when Belar attacked it next with the pestle. He slid it closer again. The herbs were powder, fine and colorless as dust, but he needed something to do with his hands. It helped him think. It helped him pretend everything was as it should be.

"All right. If it means so much to you, I'll attempt to stop her killing you until you've said what you need to. I can't promise more than that though," Cassian said. He sounded sincere in his inscrutable way.

"Thank you."

A soft touch brushed his chin. Belar flinched before he realized Cassian was only trying to get his attention. Belar let his head be turned until their gaze met. "And when we've finished with this, I'd like to kiss you again, if I may, so please do try not to die."

The words had the effect they always did. Belar's mouth went dry and a pulse of heat started deep in his chest. He meant to look away. Instead he looked down to where Cassian's lips were already forming that familiar bow.

Oh, why not?

He was very likely going to die anyway.

Belar smiled, bright and lethal. "Why wait?"

Cassian's hands found his hips, his hair, undoing the careful twist like magic so it fell around Belar's shoulders in a curtain. The hairpin clattered to the floor. It didn't matter. All that mattered was the mouth on his, the slide of their tongues, drawing out this moment's pleasure and letting it cover all the things he didn't want to feel. Not yet. He just needed one moment of peace. This was the next best thing.

Belar tasted blood. His lip throbbed lightly where he'd nicked it on Cassian's fang but that was all right too.

"You really are delicious," Cassian murmured. His tongue swept over the cut and he groaned. "I want to taste you more." Black was creeping into the corners of his eyes again. His nails felt sharp against Belar's hip.

Belar shuddered against him, pressing forward. He wanted that too. Feared it and wanted it in equal measure. He had ever since the vampire had shown up in his sitting room.

Cassian's mouth went to his neck, lips moving against the pulse as if in prayer, as if there was magic in Belar's veins.

Belar put a hand against Cassian's chest. "Wait."

It only took gentle pressure before Cassian raised his head, blinking dazed black and gold eyes at him. "What? What is it?" His voice sounded husky. He listed slightly forward, drawn to the promise of a willing pulse.

"I just thought of something. A better plan. Or part of one at least," Belar said. He grabbed up a clean knife and pricked his thumb with it. It was sharp. Sharper than any of his. The blood beaded up immediately, bright and red as summer berries. Cassian's nostrils flared. Instead of offering it to him, Belar sucked hard at the cut until his whole mouth tasted metallic and sharp. The vampire's disappointed noise quickly turned to a moan as their lips met in another kiss. His tongue sweeping into Belar's mouth, chasing the tang of blood. He bent Belar backward until he was nearly lying across the table. When they finally pulled apart again, Belar was breathless.

"That was sudden," Cassian said, licking at his lips to collect whatever blood remained. A delirious little smile curved his mouth. His hands tightened on Belar's hips. "Though not unwelcome."

"It was part of a spell." Belar blushed. The kiss had been an addition of his own making, of course. Because he'd wanted to. Because he liked the way Cassian held him, like he was everything. Like he might never let go. When Cassian touched him he felt...right. Good.

"If they're all like that you can bespell me whenever you like."

"Good, because I'm not done yet."

More blood welled up on his thumb when he pressed. He spread it across first one of Cassian's cheeks and then the other, holding Cassian's head still when he tried to turn and pull the thumb into his mouth instead. Every part of Belar was already alive with sensation. Quivering. He couldn't remember the last time he'd quivered over anyone either.

"Are you going to tell me what you're doing?" Cassian asked. He'd stopped trying to get at Belar's thumb, but Cassian hadn't let go of his hips and that was nearly as distracting. His thumbs had taken up residence just over the jut of bone on either side and the little circles they were making only served to remind him of where else they could be touching. There were so many places they hadn't gotten to yet.

Each one seemed to be crying out for immediate attention.

"I'm giving us back the element of surprise," Belar said. "Once I'm finished with you, she won't be able to see you coming." He dislodged Cassian's hands with regret and sat back on the table to inspect his work. He'd never glamoured anyone besides himself and there was every chance this wouldn't work. A full-grown vampire was more difficult than a rose.

Belar smiled as confidently as he was able. It would work. It had to.

When he'd finished, with only the blanket of his will needed to complete the glamour, Cassian encircled Belar's wrist with one hand and met his eyes. "May I?" At Belar's nod, the vampire's tongue flicked out to lave against the pad of his injured thumb. "Don't worry, I'll be gentle."

"I don't want you to be."

Cassian's expression turned wicked. He held Belar's hand in place as he collected the blood from his finger and moved his attention to his palm. He pressed kisses along the lines at its center. His eyes never left Belar's face. "I think I could love you."

Belar tried to yank his hand back. Cassian was prepared for that. The grip on his wrist wasn't tight enough to bruise, but it didn't loosen either. Trapped. Again. "Is that so terrible?" Cassian asked. His eyes practically glowed.

"I tried to kill you."

"Thrice at least, yes." His mouth and his fangs were within a breath of Belar's wrist now.

Belar felt like his heart was trying to tear free of his body. Its beating must be audible even to human ears by now. "And you barely know me."

"I like what I do know."

Lips swept skin. Belar's eyelids fluttered nearly closed. He was so distracted he didn't immediately realize that Cassian had released him. "You needn't say anything right now. But consider it," Cassian said. "If you wish."

Belar slid off the table and back to his feet. He was already considering it, had been for some time, and he still had no answer beyond the yearning deep in his chest and the fear it would disappear like a mirage. "I will." His hand sought the axe lying on the table behind him. It was heavier than his, but the weight comforted him. "But Scylla first."

Best to take things one at a time.

*

Birds chirped haltingly, hidden in nearby trees along the lane as Belar and Cassian stepped out of the front door of the house and onto the stoop. Dawn couldn't be far away if the birds were already singing, but the sky overhead was still deep blue and every house along the street was silent and dark. And there, lurking just at the end of the front walk, was a patch of deeper shadow, hardly visible at all until Belar focused on it. He still wasn't sure how something could be so completely empty and alive at the same time.

Erathel had assured them that she knew how to stabilize the shadow enough to be used as a door, but to Belar it looked no different. He would just have to trust that she knew what she was doing. For Cassian's sake if not his own. She'd shed no tears over Belar's loss.

"If that leads to the shadow realm as I suspect, you won't be able to return until nightfall," Erathel said, voice drifting through the open doorway. She had stopped at the center of the long carpet runner in the front hallway and showed no signs of going any further. "We'll expect you back then."

Arakiel had draped himself in the doorway, leaning in such a way that he was framed neatly without crossing the threshold of the house. One of his trailing sleeves fluttered over the invisible barrier. His eyes followed it.

"And if we're not?" Cassian raised an eyebrow, but there was an edge of fondness in his dry tone.

Arakiel's mouth curled into a smile with too many teeth.

Cassian nodded, almost smiling back.

"Take care, little hunter," Arakiel said.

Then Cassian took Belar's hand and they stepped into the void.

Chapter Eleven

Stepping into the shadow had been like a sudden drop into a pond Belar hadn't known was there. The sensation of free-falling before he was enveloped and then: cold. Everything was cold. Squeezing his lungs. Turning every nerve to ice. Cold so acute his muscles knotted. It forced itself down his throat and choked off his cry of pain. There was no air, just the icy dark enveloping him, so he let go and let it take him. There really wasn't any other choice.

It was a while before he realized the feeling had faded and he could breathe again. His axe had been stripped from his back. Cassian's hand was gone from his though he knew he must be close. Everything around him was twilight dark.

He was in some sort of long gallery. The walls were a tangled web, gaps between letting in only a faint amber light from whatever lay beyond. Belar moved closer to the wall, reaching out one hand to help guide him. It was so cold it felt damp to the touch. Almost slick. Not exactly stone or wood. He probably didn't want to know what it was. Everything about this place felt like a nightmare just out of reach.

When Cassian had referred to the shadow realm Belar hadn't fully appreciated what that meant. He had pictured something dark and dismal but, at its heart, familiar. Just as all chairs were inherently similar. Or cities. Architecture might change. The color of the sky or the scents in the air varied. But a chair was a chair and a city was a city. No matter how different they were, they were also the same. He'd thought a realm was a realm too.

He was wrong.

It was not like that at all.

Every movement came with the weight of stone. He could breathe, yes, but only in shallow gasps. And no matter how long he stood and waited, his eyes never adjusted to the darkness. It was like moving through a dream except here he had no control over anything. There was no waking up from this fantasy.

He pressed close to an uneven crack in the wall and peered out. Beyond he could just make out the darker lines of something tall arcing up into the sky. Trees possibly, though they had the more languid frothy shape of seaweed and they chattered and shook in the faint breeze, roots lost in the darkness below and tops nearly invisible against the expanse of the sepia sky. There were no stars. The faint shadow of something that might have been clouds streaked across it in great whorls, but if there was a moon, he couldn't see it. And far in the distance was the shimmer of light. A city? Did they have cities? Or was it a fire just out of sight?

He felt like a princess trapped in a tower. Everything seemed so far away. So strange.

What did the Fae lands look like, he wondered. Were they the reverse of this, all lightness and beauty and warmth? Or were they just as strange? Just as unwelcoming? He didn't think he ever wanted to find out.

Belar stepped back and chafed his arms with both hands, but the chill didn't dissipate. With it came the wintery numbness he had learned to expect. His fingertips felt burned by their brush with the wall. His toes were stone. He was only surprised his breath didn't cloud in the air.

Beyond the knotted walls something moved with the quiet susurrus of scales sliding against each other, but when he looked there was nothing to see. Only the same near perfect darkness that made everything look blurry and gray. Every other color had been drained out of the world.

He hurried on.

There was every possibility that he was going in the wrong direction—they all looked much the same—but he let his instincts guide him. He always did in times like these. More rustling, skittering sounds followed him through the dark, invisible to his eyes but no more comforting for it.

It was with relief that he finally came out into a new gallery. The firelight illuminating it was nearly blinding in its suddenness.

The walls were just as broken, fitted together in an uneven lattice showing slips of the empty sky outside. The wind howled through the gaps and made the fire in the braziers lining the walls throw up sparks in orange showers. There were fires everywhere making the heavy air even heavier with smoke, but none of the warmth lingered. The wind whipped it away almost immediately. Belar looked up and nearly gasped. The sky arced overhead, uninterrupted by any kind of ceiling, huge and liquid, shimmering russet and topaz where those strange clouds moved over it. He almost didn't mind the lack of stars if he could view it like this. Like gold dust suspended in oil. Close enough to touch and yet so very far away. He tore his gaze away with an effort.

At one end of the space before him—he could hardly call it a room—a circle of lanterns splashed light in a nervous dance as the wind caught them, illuminating slips of crumbling wall and molten shadow that slithered over itself. More shadows like the one that had brought him here. Belar could still feel its eyeless attention focused on him. At the center of the ring sat a form on an ornate and high-backed chair. It looked at first to be stone, but as he drew closer, he could tell it wasn't. There was something earthy about it, reminiscent of gnarled roots. Funny how there would be something like that here. It put him in mind of his father. Or how Belar had always imagined him to be whenever he had taken the time. In his musings, Belar's father always sat on something like a throne. Faceless but regal. Untouchable by time. Untouchable by humanity. Untouchable by him.

"I can see you lurking over there even in the dark. There's no hiding here. Don't be shy." The words echoed—he didn't know how since there didn't seem enough to the walls around him to make it possible—from an unseen mouth as Scylla raised an arm and beckoned him forward.

It wasn't until Belar's feet began to move on their own that he realized it hadn't been an invitation at all. It was a command. He could feel it like hooks digging into flesh. Not painful but impossible to ignore. A reminder that this was her domain. He wanted to fight it. But he had come to talk, maybe even to bargain. He let her word take him.

The floor was crumbling as badly as the rest of the place and he had to watch his footing. Black gaps between stones could have been missing tiles or holes through to whatever lay beneath. He didn't want to risk it.

Out of the corner of his eye he noticed *things* shifting, chittering in an insectile way as they passed him. He could finally identify them for what they were. More shadows. With this many together they whispered in a multitude of voices. It sounded like the lapping of waves.

As she waited for his approach, Scylla sat perfectly still. Only her dark claws moved, tapping against the arm of her knotted throne. The sound carried as clearly as her voice had.

When he'd gotten as close as he intended to, Belar bobbed an awkward curtsy. "I believe you've been looking for me."

The gloom still hid her eyes, but he sensed her gaze on him. He wasn't sure how vampires managed to do that, but it seemed to be a skill they all shared. "Is that what I've been doing?" He *could* see her fangs as she bared her teeth. Those were quite clear, but not as shocking as they would have been a few days ago. Arakiel spent so much time snarling prettily that Belar had started to build up an immunity. "Looking for you." *Click, click* went her nails. "What a clever way of putting it. Did you present yourself here only so you could beg for your life with your clever words? I might consider it. For a moment at least. It's been centuries since I've been entertained. Tell me, human, how *are* you at begging?"

There was something about her that was too big for the space she filled, as though everything around her became smaller just by her nearness, Belar included. As Belar passed into the circle of lantern light, she leaned forward.

Finally, he saw her eyes. The sclera was deep black with only the thinnest sliver of gold iris, tinted red by the lantern's glow, showing around the pupil. He could almost see himself reflected in them. Her thick rope of white hair sat over her shoulder, snaking down almost to her feet and bound with gold rings. She was clothed, but in no manner Belar had ever seen before. The garment looked ragged, like a strip of moss torn from the forest floor and fashioned into a tunic. The sharp points of her shoulders rose from the slashed openings at the sides. This close up it was obvious she had recently risen from a long rest just as Cassian had said. There was a languor to her movements. Everything about her looked exhausted. Her skin was stretched taut. Her cheekbones stood out in stark relief, ready to slice through that fragile layer of flesh, thin as onion skin.

Click, click, click.

"Oh, I hadn't planned on begging. I assume it would be useless and it's not really in my nature, you understand. But you went to so much trouble to set me up, I thought I should pay you a visit at the very least." He looked up at her through his lashes as he bowed again. "If you wanted me to kill someone for you, all you had to do was hire me," Belar said. The lanterns were close behind him. They tolled like funeral bells on their chains.

"Why would I wish to hire *you*? You who killed my son."

And there it was. All snapping teeth and malice.

She didn't move and her expression didn't change but he could feel her readiness. One unwary word and he would be missing a head.

"It would have been easier, for one thing," he said. And now he would have to kill her. A shard of disappointment pierced his heart. He'd meant what he said to Cassian before. He didn't *enjoy* the killing. But he didn't enjoy the idea of dying either.

Scylla sat back, crossing one leg over the other. Her eyes pinned him in place. "Easy. Was it easy when you murdered my son? How did you do it? You humans always go for the head, do you not? You're too weak any other way." She smiled as her jab hit the mark and Belar stiffened. "Besides, what use have I for you when I have a human of my own already? Not human for much longer though, I fear. Such a pity. They never last. He has been quite useful."

"What? Who?"

"Not so clever now, are we? You didn't know?" She raised pale eyebrows, mouth a mocking pucker.

He hadn't. They'd been so focused on finding the reason behind everything that he'd never stopped to work out the how. It seemed like such an obvious mistake now. The human who Demetria had mentioned had entirely slipped his mind. Now Belar pushed the thought away like the distraction it was. He couldn't do anything about it while he was here. One thing at a time.

He looked up at Scylla. She still seemed enormous, but he was growing accustomed to it. And it really didn't matter how big or small she was. He would do what he had to do. He always had.

Out of the corner of his eye he saw movement. At first, he took it for another shadow. Scylla didn't notice it slipping along the edges of the room toward her throne. Good to see his glamour was still working as it should. For once.

"I don't expect I can frighten you into relenting, but I wish you would reconsider this," Belar said. "Please. No one else needs to die."

She stared at him for a long time in silence before the tapping of her fingers finally stilled. "On the contrary. Some need it very much. Where is the other one? Cassian. Somehow he got free of my shadow. Death will be a favor for him, I think. More than he even deserves." When Belar didn't answer, she went on. "Or have you been abandoned? They do that. The kin. They did it to my Dismas, tossed him away like trash for one mistake, and they would do the same to you. If you lived long enough."

"Dismas drained an entire town in a week," he said flatly. It was a night he didn't like to recall, walking through a street of discarded corpses to put the vampire to the axe. They'd found him smiling, mouth still sticky with blood, and he had laughed and laughed. Belar still dreamed about it sometimes when the nights were long and he was alone. In those dreams, things didn't always end in his favor.

And she waved her hand like it was nothing. "Humans."

He barely took a step before they caught him by the arms. Cold fingers of shadow wrapped tight around his wrists and any attempts at struggling only made them pull harder, dragging him almost to his knees on the cracked floor.

Well, shit.

The atmosphere in this place was harder on him than he had expected, but it wasn't anything he couldn't work around. He had to. He refused to die this way.

"Finished begging so soon?" She tipped her head at him. "I expected a little more effort before you gave up."

Belar grinned. The effort of staying upright was already straining his muscles. His shoulders were screaming. But he made sure to look her right in the eye as something slid behind her throne, dark against dark. About fucking time. "Sorry to disappoint."

He dropped. The silver knife he'd hidden in his boot sliced through the tangled fingers of the shadows holding him, dissipating the nearest wisps, as he rolled sideways and into a crouch. It wouldn't get rid of them for long, but he only needed a moment anyway. Beside the throne his axe hung suspended in Cassian's glamoured hands just before he swung it into a wide arc. The movement rippled through the glamour, sloughing it off in waves, darkness peeling back to show his true form. He had begun to shift again. His gloved hands were too long; sharp clawed fingers straining the leather. His bared teeth were all points.

Mid-swing he stopped as though he'd hit an invisible barrier. Cassian flew backward. The axe fell from his grasp before he hit the wall with a sick thud. Belar was halfway to him when his foot stuck to the floor again. Shadows climbed his legs like vines.

Scylla had barely moved. It had only taken a wave of her hand to stop Cassian. She turned back to Belar. "That's all? I have to say I'm underwhelmed. I expected better from the human who killed my son. Perhaps I expect too much."

Belar shrugged the best he could while still bound in shadows. "Give me back my axe and I can try again."

Her smile held too many edges. “Oh no no no. We’re done playing. I had planned to draw this out a bit longer, but I have such a thirst. Don’t worry. I’ll leave enough of your body so they know whom to mourn. Come here, human.” She leaned forward on her throne, both hands stretching out to receive him, and Belar was dragged forward, knees grating over the floor as he tried to get free. The shadow creatures were around him in ropes, pinning his arms against his sides as they bore him up. Closer and closer. With this many together they felt cold. Solid. He tried kicking at the nearest clump. His foot sank in and stayed there.

Close up Scylla had a little of the same rotting earth smell of the shadow beasts and her fingers were like barbs where they touched him, each clawed tip piercing his arm in a line as the shadows released him into her grasp. She held him struggling and on his knees before her throne. When he looked up into her face, the paler ring of her irises were almost swallowed up by the black within and without. There was something hollow about her gaze, like only a portion of her was looking at him. Maybe the rest was still dreaming somewhere.

She traced one talon from his forehead down to the tip of his nose. He kept very still. Even that gentle pressure was enough to slice him open. “If I wasn’t so thirsty, I might turn you, too, let you lose yourself to my service just like your friend before you. But I don’t think there will be enough of you left for that. I would have liked to have seen it.” She licked her lips.

"I am sorry things have come to this," Belar whispered. "I don't suppose that makes it any better."

She tilted her head curiously.

Belar held up the vial he had palmed along with his knife. Light exploded out between his fingers as he crushed it, brighter than any flare he'd made before, flaming up in his palm, through his arm. It was like touching the sun, so bright it dazzled his eyes even closed. The beasts around them screeched as they burned. Scylla threw up both hands to shield herself, a scream like winter wind howling out of her. Belar stumbled back. But he didn't fall. Cassian was there waiting. One arm held over his face. He set the axe in Belar's hand and stumbled back.

"I'm sorry," Belar said as he swung. "I really am."

*

The silence rang for a long time after in the empty room. Scylla had crumbled to ash at the end, a testament to her age perhaps, and had slowly sifted to the floor and faded away. There was nothing left now but the gash where the axe had bitten into her throne and the silence.

And them.

Belar dropped to the floor, the axe laying at his side. He didn't want to touch it. Not yet. His hand throbbed with a hundred points of pain from the vial he'd crushed, glass shards embedded in his palm, and the heat of it had left him feeling raw. A line of punctures ran along his arm from her claws. It was likely they would scar. Vampire wounds often did.

The flare still fizzed with intermittent light where he had dropped it. Gold and silver sparks skittered across the floor and made the knotted walls shiver around them.

Cassian had circled around the perimeter twice already, giving him his space to be silent and still.

Nothing else moved. All the other shadows had fled or burned away.

Finally, Cassian crouched before him, arms braced on knees as he looked into Belar's face. "Can you stand?"

He could. It wasn't a question of that at all. He nodded and slowly looked around. There were at least a few back at headquarters who would have done anything to visit this place, study it. He could probably even earn a bonus if he told them. But he wouldn't of course. "Where are we? Beyond the obvious, I mean. Can we get back?"

"To the first: that's not a question I can answer in any way you'd understand. To the second: it's some hours yet before night falls and the door opens again. But we're safe enough here. Anything that saw your light will probably stay away for a while." He paused. "And thank you."

Belar arched an eyebrow.

"It may not feel especially noble at the moment, but you did save my life as well as your own. That's worth a little gratitude, don't you think?"

He nodded. Exhaustion wrapped around him like clouds and when Cassian dropped down beside him Belar let himself be pulled closer. He slowly dropped until his head was pillowed on Cassian's thigh. Overhead the perpetually night sky swirled. A shape, darker and blacker, moved over it. The body was long and eel-like save for the flare of wide fins. Or wings. Its low bellows were echoed by other, unseen, creatures. Belar followed it with his eyes until the high wall blocked his view.

"What did she mean?"

Cassian looked at him quizzically.

"About turning me. Could she really have made me into one of you?"

"Ah." His lips pursed. "No." Most of his expression was obscured at this angle, but Belar caught his grimace. "It's the favorite lie of some kin, but there is no way to turn a human into a vampire that I have ever heard of. One can...shift them into something in between, not quite shadow, not quite mortal. When the change is complete it leaves them beholden to the one who made them and with very little will of their own. As you've seen."

At first Belar didn't know what he meant. Then he remembered those dark eyes peering at him from across his yard. "The shadow beasts."

"Yes."

Belar felt ill. "That's terrible."

Cassian didn't deny it, only nodded again. He raised his head to look up at the sky. "Rest a while. I'll wake you when night comes."

"How will you know?"

"I'll know."

Belar was too tired to argue so he closed his eyes, removing his spectacles and handing them to Cassian for safekeeping. It was miraculous that they hadn't broken during the fight.

Cassian took Belar's hand in his and began methodically picking the shards of glass from his palm. He flicked each one aside with a pointed claw before working at the next. When he'd finished, he laved the skin with a flat tongue until it tingled and sometime between that and night Belar drifted off to sleep.

Chapter Twelve

Belar woke in the luxurious embrace of a bed—which was becoming familiar after several days—and with early sun streaming in the window—which was not. He put up a hand to cover his eyes and cried out at the jolt of pain the movement brought. It ran all down his arm and through the muscles of his back. He held still for a moment and let the muscles unknot before he shifted to look at his hand. It was neatly bandaged and smelled faintly of some kind of herbal salve. Lavender maybe.

The door clicked quietly open, and a short, fat person inserted themself into the room. "Oh good, you're awake." Their face cracked into a self-conscious smile before they came closer. "This house can get a little creepy during the day with everyone else asleep. It breathes. You understand."

Belar sat up to squint at them, wincing again at the chain of pinches and pulls set off by the movement.

"That's right, your spectacles! I have them here. They were a little bent. I fixed that too." They patted their pockets before producing the gold frames.

When they were offered, Belar snatched the person's wrist instead and pulled. They tipped forward with a startled squawk and almost fell onto the bed. "Who are you? What are you doing here?" Belar groped behind him with his free hand but only came up with a fistful of sheets. The least someone could have done was leave him a knife beneath the pillow.

"I-I'm Percy?" They said it like they expected Belar to argue. Their eyes were a bright clear blue, wide now with shock, but no fear. Belar released their wrist and they straightened up again, fixing their crooked shirt front. There was no tie or waistcoat over it and the sleeves had been rolled to the elbows. "I suppose you must be surprised to see me here. I've bandaged you up twice now, but you were asleep both times, so we haven't even met properly. Despite"—they waved a hand, cheeks going slightly pink—"my having seen you in a state." They held out a hand to shake before remembering Belar's injured hand. They presented the opposite hand for him to take instead.

Belar still had no idea to whom he was speaking. Or why he had reacted that way. He wasn't in the business of protecting vampires from...whoever this Percy was. They looked harmless—not a fang or a claw in sight—but he had a hard time trusting that. Anyone permitted to wander a vampire's house was hardly going to be average.

Belar took the offered hand. Percy nodded when Belar gave his name. They made a thoughtful noise. "I've heard a little about you. I'm the gardener. And imagine my surprise when I arrived to tend the plants and they shoved an unconscious man at me. I thought you were *dead* the first time. Near fell over in a panic since I'm not qualified to fix *that*. I'm used to it now though. You seem to be very injury prone." Percy perched at the foot of the bed while Belar put on his spectacles and peered at them. They looked much the same as they had when still blurry. Still a little round everywhere except their hands—which were squarish, the short nails with a little dirt beneath them. Their skin was a sun-warmed tan and loose curls of brown hair fell about their temples despite an attempt at oiling it into submission.

"You're the gardener?" Erathel had said something about them but the ache creeping into Belar's head made it hard to concentrate long enough to pry out the memory.

Percy nodded. "Hedge witchery runs in my family, but there's not much money in that these days. A person has to make a living. Vampires are good for business as long as you don't mind the odd hours. Which I don't." They grinned impishly.

Despite himself, Belar was charmed.

He stretched, things popping and cracking all over his body from the long rest he'd had. Finally, his eyes fell on the lump in the corner. Cassian slumped in the chair stationed beside the windows, fast asleep, the curtains blocking any sun that might have disturbed him. It was the first time Belar had seen a vampire sleep and truth be told it was a little underwhelming. Cassian looked just like an ordinary human with his eyes closed, sprawled in a chair wearing the rumpled and stained shirt he'd been in the night before. The stains looked worse in this light than they had in the gloom of the shadow realm. There were even faint snores coming from his parted lips.

"He's been there all night," Percy said, following his gaze.

"I didn't think he slept at all."

Percy shrugged.

Belar watched the sleeping vampire for another minute before he creakily made his way out of the bed. He wanted nothing more than to sleep for weeks, but he'd made the mistake of ignoring evidence once already, and the things Scylla had said to him grew louder the longer he was awake. "I need clothes."

The wardrobe along the wall was now filled with an assortment of borrowed clothing in his size. The parcels from Marisol's shop had been stacked along the bottom, still unopened. The topmost was unfamiliar. A cream envelope had been tucked into the wide ribbon holding it closed. Belar tugged it free and broke the seal.

Wear it well, said the note in a neat hand. And beneath Marisol's elaborate signature a postscript read, *We embellished a bit. You won't mind.*

"What's that?" Percy whispered from behind him.

Belar passed over the note.

Inside the wrapping lay a coat similar to one of the ones he had tried at the shop—this one midnight-blue—but where it had been beautiful before, now it was fantastical. The cut was full in the skirts and the lapels had been embroidered with leaves in silvery thread. The motif was repeated in even more detail down the back, forked branches and narrow pointed leaves spreading down to the hem in delicate sprays before wrapping back around to the front. Here and there darker threads swirled into the rest in the suggestion of clouds flitting over a night sky. Fitting after where he'd just been. Belar ran a reverent hand down the sleek fabric of the impossible coat. It should have taken weeks to finish. It must have cost an immense amount of money, even more so to compensate for the speed with which the embroidery had been accomplished, and he wanted it more than he'd wanted nearly any other thing in the world.

He felt a near physical pain as he set the package back in the wardrobe and reached for the plain shirt and coat instead. Cassian had called it payment for services rendered at the time, but it didn't feel like that. It felt like being indebted.

"Aren't you going to wake him?" Percy asked.

Belar shucked his torn trousers and Percy made a startled peep. When Belar glanced back, the hedge witch had shifted on the bed so they were facing away toward the window. "I should be back before sundown. Let him sleep. There's something I need to do, and it can't wait."

"And if he asks where you've gone?"

Belar smiled. "Tell him...I used the door this time instead of the window."

*

Headquarters was just as barren as Belar could have hoped. Even the lights had gone dim since there wasn't anyone present to require them. They flickered back to life one by one, leading the way, as Belar crept down the hallway and let himself into Merriville's office.

Belar *tsked* in annoyance. The door wasn't even locked. The man was just asking to be burgled, in which case Belar was happy to assist.

Finding out someone had tampered with his files, that they had manipulated him into performing their assassinations for him, had nearly stripped away whatever peace Belar had in this job, but he had wanted to preserve the last scrap of hope that it had been a vampire or some other shadowy being. No one he knew. No one he had exchanged words with, smiled at, even as they were going behind his back. Scylla's words had taken that away from him too. Someone he knew had helped her, willingly or not. He just needed to find some kind of proof.

The files in Merriville's office were more disorganized than the archives, heaped in piles atop the shelves and stacked on the corner of his desk. It was a wonder Merriville got anything done if this was how he kept his office. A mess didn't even begin to describe it. Belar unearthed at least three case files from a year ago while he was searching for his own. They should have been toward the top if Merriville had done as he'd said and reviewed them after Belar's request. But he couldn't find them. Belar sorted through each of the piles in growing confusion before moving on to the shelves. Duplicate files were burned, but these should have remained since they were only a few months old and Merriville was obviously so far behind on his review.

Belar pulled out another thick file and undid the tie, this from last winter. Another was from spring. Finally, Belar spotted his own neat handwriting on a tag and yanked the file free. Inside was the final report from his last haunting. He threw it down in the center of Merriville's desk where he couldn't help but notice it.

"Do your filing, damn you."

He locked the door to the office on his way back out, feeling defeated, before heading to the archives. Merriville would have been the neatest culprit, but with his office in such a state it was more likely that Merriville hadn't even *seen* Belar's reports. It was a wonder he even got the payments out on time.

Which meant Belar would have to do this the old-fashioned way. He had rooted out plenty of targets for this job over the years. He had just never expected to find himself up to his elbows in hunters' files. They were supposed to be locked after all. And in theory they were. The door to the section of the archive that held all their personal files was bolted with a special lock and bore a sign saying No Admittance in stiff black letters. Belar had been inside only once, just to see if he could without some silent alarm alerting everyone to his transgression. He'd stood there a long time. Waiting. No one had even known. And they never would. He'd swiped the spare key when he was still a new recruit and Merriville had given up looking for the original and had a new one made ages ago. Lucky for Belar they were bad about changing the locks.

The key turned easily, and he let himself into the airless room. It was more of a closet. The only illumination came from a single hanging light and the corners were thick with grime and shadows. He wondered when anyone had last cleaned in here since only four people—one of them Merriville—were allowed in according to the sign on the door. None of those people were the custodians.

Belar crossed to the drawers and began pulling files in search of the addresses he needed. Headquarters never stayed empty for long. He could come up with a lie to explain his presence in the one place he wasn't supposed to be, but it was always better not to be seen at all.

Whoever had set him up knew his schedule with some degree of accuracy. Possible with some of the newer hunters but less likely. Location made no substantial difference—he wasn't the only senior hunter who could come and go as they pleased—but it certainly wouldn't hurt either. Which left only two likely candidates and he couldn't bear the thought of Marta doing all this to him. It was foolishly sentimental of him. He knew it. But when he left headquarters, he still went to the other address on his list first.

Horace had earned a visit.

*

Horace had let a tiny place in a boarding house on the shabby side of town, which was surprisingly close to the vampire side of town, Belar now realized. It consisted of only two rooms: a bedroom with blank walls, no curtains, and a creaky brass bed and a sitting room that looked like it saw only marginally more use. A dented kettle sat atop the wood stove in the corner, both cold. The sight of a typewriter on a rickety table hit like a knife in his stomach. Surely people had typewriters for other reasons, despite the expense. Abundant letter writing, for instance.

Or...

He couldn't think of an "or."

A stack of papers sat nearby. Belar grabbed the top sheet and fed it into the machine, turning the platen until it was secured in place so he could tap out a string of Hs. They were without the flaw of the machine at headquarters. Hardly solid evidence. But the paper was.

He had initially taken the papers for cast-offs. He really hadn't wanted to believe it. Despite everything he hadn't. He turned over the next paper on the stack.

They weren't cast-offs. They were reports.

He tore the page from the typewriter and scanned it. His own notes, some of them misaligned and askew in his agitation, stared back at him. The page had once belonged to his last report. He crumpled the paper and threw it aside.

He hadn't expected the truth to hurt.

Belar threw himself at the chair beside the window and settled in to wait. He had no idea what else Horace did to make ends meet, but hopefully it wouldn't keep him too long. The day was already half over. Belar wanted to be back by nightfall as he'd promised.

Somehow, he managed to doze anyway as exhaustion caught up with him once more. He woke to twilight creeping into the sky and the rattle of the doorknob.

Horace stopped in the doorway before stepping inside and closing the door behind him. He looked thinner again, stubble lining his jaw, and dark smudges under his eyes. "I didn't think we were friends enough for social calls," he said.

"We're not. How did Scylla get you? I hope she paid you well to fuck me over," Belar said in the same flat tone. He tapped out an even beat on the arms of the chair, counting the rest until Horace spoke.

"What do you think?" As the sun faded from the window the shadows seemed to collect around him, but mostly in his eyes, darkening them until their brown was eaten up by black. They weren't the reflective mirror of vampire eyes. They never would be. What Belar saw in them was an echo of the empty black stare he'd seen across his yard the night Cassian had come to him.

Belar stood, slowly, hands up to show he had no weapons. "Whatever she offered, it was lies. You're not going to become a vampire. You might be something, but it won't be like them."

Horace laughed. It sounded hollow. "Thank you for the sudden concern. I didn't know you cared, Belar. I'm touched. Really. And I don't *care,* you ass; don't you get it? I should have been dead months ago when that thing tore me open, but here I am. And here I'm staying." He held up a fist that suddenly looked burnt black and uncurled clawed fingers. He flexed his hand again before he looked back at Belar and smiled. "This is good. Powerful. I like it."

"You hate me that much?"

"Don't flatter yourself. I worked for years, saving people who never even knew my name, never cared, never bothered to say thank you, and for what? So Merriville could shuffle me off on leave and forget the first chance he got? I rescued five people that day and he treated it like an embarrassment. I chose me. You didn't even enter the picture," Horace snorted. He bared teeth that were longer than they should have been, gray lips peeling back like the skin on rotten fruit. "We're all of us on our own. And no one will miss you when you're gone either."

Horace's head cocked to one side, bones and joints cracking in a way that should have been painful, but he gave no sign. His shirt cuffs pulled back to expose forearms covered in coarse cadaverous gray skin. But his eyes were the worst. Dark as wells. They threatened to pull him in.

Horace lunged. The moment shattered as his claws tore the air and Belar tipped backward. He threw up an arm to shield his throat.

The blow never fell.

Horace's eyes widened. He seemed to hang suspended, mouth drooping open. Something crunched. A black hole gaped where his heart should have been, the raw ends of bone edging the wound like lace. Cassian straightened and pulled his bloodied hand free from Horace's chest, letting him drop to the floor at his feet.

"I beg to differ on that last point," Cassian said. He shook his hand out, streaked with too-dark blood that splattered over the floor, and then pulled a handkerchief from his pocket. "I would miss him. Quite a lot."

Horace wheezed. His hands twitched against the floor before he lay still again. His body collapsed in on itself, the ruined ribcage falling inward and the flesh crisping until there was little more than a gray husk left.

Cassian worked the last bit of the blood from between his fingers and then laid the soiled handkerchief over what remained of Horace's face. It hardly looked like him anymore, angles and features pulled out of shape by the unfinished change. Cassian searched Belar's face. "Are you all right?"

"A little tired of everyone trying to kill me, if I'm being honest." He tried on a wan smile. "How did you even find me? And here of all places?"

Cassian smiled. "I did promise to protect you from the shadows. I believe this makes us even. Our truce is ended." He stepped gingerly around the body on the floor. "Though I had hoped to make a new one. If you're agreeable."

Belar met his eyes. He really should have been more concerned about the dead man, about the fact he could have torn Belar's throat out before he drew his knife and very nearly had, but the truth was none of that was particularly remarkable in his line of work. Something or someone would probably be trying to kill him again by tomorrow. But the way Cassian was looking at him, the way it made warmth curl in Belar's chest, *that* at least was new.

So, he said, "What kind of bargain did you have in mind?" His gaze dropped to the floor. "Though we should take care of him first. I don't know Horace's landlady, but whoever she is I doubt she deserves to come back to this."

And apparently there would always be a mess to clean up.

Chapter Thirteen

Normality was a strange thing.

They had used a sheet off Horace's bed as a shroud and taken the body away to burn. Whatever combination of stubborn will and magic had held him together over the last year had vanished at his death. Without it all that remained was a crumbling shell. His brittle bones had shattered from the simple act of transporting them to an empty lot where the fire would go unnoticed. Belar hardly had to light a match. He was already gone. Dust.

If there were any questions around headquarters about Horace's sudden disappearance, Belar hadn't heard them. He planned to keep it that way. An absence of people or things trying to kill him meant he was back on leave where he belonged.

And not a moment too soon either.

The first snows came early this year. After he recovered enough from his fight with Scylla to travel, Belar had gone home to finish his recovery in peace. Cassian had tried to dissuade him, but it was too difficult to relax in the vampires' dark house.

He needed to be alone. To think. To test his feelings and see if they still held once the danger had passed.

He hadn't so much fled as tactfully retreated, he reasoned.

Belar had barely gotten in the door of his almost too quiet cottage before everything was blanketed in white as soft as velvet. Looking out at the frost-tipped pines and the quiet lull of activity in the streets it was difficult to believe any of it had happened. Cassian, his strange cousins, and their even stranger house seemed like something out of a fever dream even knowing everything he did, even *doing* what he did.

Belar turned away from the window.

"Why don't we try that one more time from the beginning, Millicent," he said, flicking out the long skirts of his coat so he wouldn't crush the fabric as he sat on the piano bench at her side. "But this time I'll play the bass, you the treble. I want you to focus on an even tempo. Can you do that?"

Millicent kicked her legs, tongue poking out of the corner of her mouth. "I think so." She slid forward on the bench and stretched one foot out in a vain pursuit of the sustain pedal.

"I'll do that part as well," Belar added quickly. If she reached much farther, she might slide right off the bench. She'd gotten taller in recent weeks, sprouting like a weed according to her mother, but it still wasn't enough to bridge the gap between her feet and the floor when she sat.

He lifted his fingers to the keys and began the count.

It wasn't terrible. Millicent rocked back and forth as she played, her small shoulder bumping his in a steady beat, and by the end Belar was biting his lip to keep from smiling. He was...happy. How strange. The thought was so distracting it took him a full minute to realize the song had ended and Millicent was gazing up at him again with brown eyes roughly the size of twin moons. "Yes?"

"You didn't say anything. You always say something," Millicent informed him seriously. Her hands were folded in her lap in an attitude of sainted patience.

"Oh. Yes. That was...very good. You've really improved these last few weeks."

Her smile took up most of her face, even squishing her eyes into cat-like slits. Then she turned to point out of the window. "There's a man standing outside waiting. He looks fancy."

Belar whipped around on the bench. The late day sun stretched shadows across the snowy yard in long blue streaks. Cassian stood in the biggest patch of shadow, leaning against the tree in the yard with his arms crossed over his chest and a sleepy smile on his face. He was dressed in a deep-green suit today with a matching capelet over his shoulders as a nod to the winter chill he barely felt.

Somehow in the weeks since Belar had last seen him, he had managed to forget how bright Cassian's eyes could be. Like liquid fire. His memory couldn't live up to the reality and it couldn't prepare him for the way his stomach clenched at the sight of the vampire. He had wondered, hoped, feared that the distance while they sorted out their own affairs would undo whatever spell they'd fallen under. It hadn't. Belar hadn't even realized he was waiting for Cassian until the wait was over and all the tension that had settled into his bones these last weeks melted away. In its place was warmth. Cassian had come back. To him.

When Cassian noticed them looking, he raised a black gloved hand and waved.

"Someone should tell him it's not nice to stare in other people's windows though."

Belar started and turned back to Millicent. "You're absolutely correct. It's very rude. I'll be sure to scold him about that later."

"Do you teach that man piano too?"

"No, not piano." He had tried—briefly—after discovering that Erathel's and Arakiel's house possessed a music room furnished with a piano that was even mysteriously in tune despite none of them knowing how to play it. Belar suspected it was just another part of their collection since he had found violins (also with no one to play them) and an entire section of the library dedicated to books in languages they couldn't read. Either way, Cassian had shown no patience for the piano and Belar was happier keeping it to himself anyway. He'd never had a piano of his own before. Even if it resided in the home of a pair of vampires who were older than he could imagine.

"Flute?"

"What? Oh, no. Not flute either." Belar stood from the bench and started collecting his things since they were nearly done for the day. "He's...he's my..." He frowned, snatched the music off the music stand of the piano, and folded the sheets together again, rather than attempting to blunder through the rest of an explanation. "I'll bring you another piece to practice next week, shall I?" When he checked, Cassian had disappeared from the window and hopefully from the conversation as well.

Millicent nodded so enthusiastically the bow in her hair bounced. Red today. Once he'd collected the rest of his things, she slid off the bench and trailed him to the door to receive her customary farewell and reminder about practicing every day while Belar wrapped himself in his topcoat and an enormous wooly scarf. Mittens after that. He smiled a little at the memory of the student—now long gone—who had knitted them for him. They were slightly too short in the thumbs, but they were thick, and they kept the ache out of his joints in the cold which made them indispensable. Millicent stayed at his side for the entire ritual before seeing him out.

Belar was halfway down the front walk when the door popped open again. "See you next week," Millicent bellowed. Belar waved as she slammed the door again. For good this time.

"You can come out now. You've already been spotted," Belar said. "And your lack of stealth is really quite disappointing from a professional standpoint. Standing under a tree in broad daylight." He clucked his tongue in mock disapproval. "You were probably spotted by half the town."

Cassian stepped out from behind the hedge bordering the front gate. He unlatched it to let Belar through and bowed. "I thought I might walk you home."

Of all the things he'd hoped the vampire might do for him, or with him, a walk of half a mile should hardly have been worth mentioning, but Belar felt nearly giddy. What was happening to him? "You came all the way here just for that?"

"Not only that, but that *is* why I'm currently braving the sun instead of finding a nice dark place to reside, yes. I wanted to see you." A faint smile touched Cassian's lips. It was followed by the light sweep of one icy thumb against Belar's cheek. He must have been standing outside for a while. From what Belar could tell, vampires didn't feel the cold in the same way he did, but they didn't seem to enjoy it much either. The chill had turned his lips pale too. "The rest can wait until later. I don't particularly want to talk about playing catch-up with the last seventy years. It makes me feel like a museum exhibit."

Belar snorted a laugh to cover the very real flutter of pleasure in his chest. "You missed my charming presence. Admit it." He smirked at Cassian.

Something bright flared in the vampire's eyes. Belar leaned into him. "I did actually," Cassian said in a low voice. His head dipped, and instantly Belar's mind was filled with memories of those last stolen and bloody kisses they had shared and the way Cassian's hands had spread over his back, like he was molding both body and pleasure to fit his design. But there was certainly a place for that, and he didn't think it was here on the street where half his neighbors could see.

Belar cleared his throat. "First, Millicent asked me to inform you of how unmannerly it is to stare into other people's windows."

Cassian fell into step with him as he set off down the road. "Is that so." It was a statement, not question.

"Indeed. You could learn much about manners from her." He bit his lip. "She also asked who you were. I suppose I should think of an answer for that. This town is very quiet. You'll be the talk of every gossip by the end of the week and so will I." As if to prove his point, a young man up the road paused at this gate to watch them pass. Belar waved cheerfully even though he had no clue who the boy was and then towed Cassian more quickly away.

The vampire tried to lace their fingers together and was momentarily confounded by the mitten before he adjusted his grip. "You can call me whatever you like if it pleases you."

"Friend?"

"Of course."

Belar caught his breath. Cassian's hand around his was an anchor. "We do work very well together. I could also tell them you're my business partner."

Cassian raised an eyebrow at that but finally nodded. "What business are we supposedly in together? In case any of your charming human neighbors get around to asking." He paused. "None of these people know what it is you do every night, do they?"

"*Absolutely* not. I would have to move. All of my students would quit me."

He planned never to let that happen, but imagining it sent a pang through him anyway. Belar lifted his gaze to the ice-crusted trees lining the road. Tattered ribbons fluttered from some of the branches, left over from the autumn festivals and trapped now until the wind tore them free. A few of the houses bore red and gold garlands. The first frost had come on so quickly that many of his neighbors were still trying to catch up to the new season. He liked this town, quiet and mundane as it was. The peace of it. The slow routine of these people he knew by name and face and reputation even if they never did more than nod across the green to each other. Whenever he finally had to move on, Belar would do so with regret.

"Was that everything on your list of options?" Cassian asked in a leading voice.

"Did you have an addition to make?"

Cassian glanced at him, one fang peeking out of his smile. "A few. I wasn't sure what kind of approach you would prefer so I thought we might start with something romantic and go on from there. I'm not familiar with how humans handle these things, so you'll have to tell me if I've got it wrong."

Romantic. Belar's mouth went dry at the word. A few months ago, he wouldn't have considered anything they had done together "romantic," but maybe that was just a failing of his own imagination. What did he know about romance anyway? He'd always thought love was supposed to be soft, delicate as early spring clouds. Too fragile to ever fit into a life spent in the dark with monsters. But whatever name could be put to this thing between him and Cassian, he liked it. It suited him in ways he hadn't dared to dream. He wanted more. He wanted as much of it as Cassian could give him for as long as he could.

Cassian went on in the silence, "I still don't need to sleep much, you see, and there's only so much of Arakiel's hobbies I can take, so I've dedicated quite a lot of that time to thinking about kissing you instead. Especially those delightful little noises you made the last time. And how I might encourage you to make them again. It's become something of a favorite pastime. I thought I might even find you on my doorstep some night so we could continue what we had started."

Belar choked on an inhale. He could almost picture it in lurid detail, right down to the smells and the tastes. The perfect tightness of Cassian's grip as he held him. "I considered it," he said in a shrinking voice.

"And?"

He retreated into the safety of his voluminous scarf to cover the flush creeping up his neck. Honesty never stopped being terrible. “I wasn’t sure I wanted to. Everything happened so fast, I needed to think about it first.”

“Because I’m a vampire?” Despite the neutral tone, Cassian looked skeptical.

Belar snorted. “If I was going to have doubts about that I would have done it before I ever kissed you. You’ll recall that was me.” He held up one mittened finger to indicate himself.

“Oh, I do.” Cassian tilted his head to meet Belar’s eyes. His smile could have swayed kings. Belar didn’t know if Cassian had always been this attractive or if he was only seeing it now because he liked the man. Not that it mattered overmuch. Belar was only too ready to be pleased by the sight of Cassian now, whatever the cause. “As I said, very fond memories.”

“I don’t often pursue things, romantically I mean. It never seemed fair when there’s every possibility I might not return from a hunt someday and they would never know why. I won’t do that to someone else. And I don’t fall into bed with people, vampire *or* human, because I don’t want to. Except now I’ve been thinking about doing both of those things. With you. To a frankly alarming degree.”

They were nearly to Belar’s cottage, the road they walked narrowing as it forked away from the main branch leading out of town. Almost to privacy. Back to where they had met again. It seemed somehow fitting.

"I alarm you now?" Cassian asked, amused.

Belar nodded to the path ahead and his cottage. The winter sun washed out the color in the blue shutters and his garden was buried under the snow. It probably looked quite a bit different than it had when Cassian had first been there, but Belar assumed he recognized it anyway. "My home is just there. You're welcome to come in and alarm me again. If you'd like."

"Are you going to throw knives at me again?" Cassian leaned down to him, mouth hovering one taunting inch away.

"I had considered it. Especially if you don't make your decision quickly."

His low voice beside Belar's ear made him shiver. "I would like nothing better."

*

The door had barely closed before Belar slammed Cassian back against it. He was still cold from the walk outside and everything about Cassian was warm and wonderful as he moved into the circle of his arms and pressed their mouths together. Everything that had happened in the city had receded into a dream-like fantasy. He wanted to remember what it was like to be held again. To see if his imagination had gotten this thing with Cassian right. He wanted...to get these fucking mittens off. Belar pulled away just long enough to yank the mittens off with his teeth and toss them after his topcoat before throwing himself back against Cassian. So far, the vampire's lips were exactly as he'd remembered. Better even because now they were finally here. On his.

Belar clung closer. If he could only crawl inside this feeling, he would be happy.

Cassian chuckled, one hand already working its way up into Belar's hair, unraveling him with every gentle tug against the roots. With the other he lifted Belar's newly bare hand to his lips and pressed a kiss to the back, then to his knuckles, his fingertips, his palm. "I've been thinking about this too," he said. The words vibrated against Belar's skin.

When Cassian's lips found the pulse at his wrist, tongue dancing lightly over it, Belar groaned. He had felt that all the way down to his toes. It wasn't fair. "What were you thinking about?"

Belar's coat slid down his arms and disappeared as Cassian propelled him backward. They collided with the side table. Cassian reached down to steady the teetering lamp without looking. "About how good you taste." He nipped at Belar's ear, nuzzled at the sensitive spot beneath. "And the way it felt when I had you on the floor." Belar had thought about that too. He was glad to know he hadn't been the only one. He clawed at the buttons of Cassian's coat, suddenly clumsy. There were too many of them. Cassian pulled his hands away and set them on his shoulders instead. "Defenseless."

"Oh stars yes." He swallowed hard.

"And what you would look like as you came. I think about that," Cassian purred. "Often." Belar's grip tightened on his shoulders. "Will you show me?"

Instead of answering he pulled Cassian's mouth back to his and wrapped both arms around his neck. He wanted that. He wanted it so badly he was shaking, wanted it so badly he was terrified.

"Hmm?" One of Cassian's hands slipped inside Belar's shirt to tug it off his shoulders. He didn't even remember unbuttoning it. Cassian mouthed at his exposed shoulder, teeth sinking in just enough to make Belar's eyes fly open again and meet Cassian's amused gaze. "Tell me what it is you want."

A firm hand ran down Belar's stomach and then stopped. So close. Another few inches and it would be right where he wanted it. Belar growled, frustrated. He dug his fingers into Cassian's hair as he kissed him. "I want to finish what we started that night. All of it."

Strong hands turned him, pulling him back again Cassian's chest. One arm wrapped around his chest, cradling his chin as he tipped Belar's head to the side and his mouth found his artery again and settled there. "I could drain you dry like this." He licked a stripe up Belar's neck as one hand moved down and cupped him through the fabric of his trousers. "And you would die happy. With a smile on your face. You would thank me, wouldn't you?"

He nodded desperately. There was no denying it. The helpless pleasure of it. The way it made him shiver. He arched forward just to feel Cassian's grip on him tighten, to keep him in place.

"You're so beautiful." Fangs scraped his skin in another gentle nip just below the first. "I won't bite you now...but maybe next time?" His lips were a warm tease.

Was it the promise of a next time or of the exquisite pain that made him shudder? "I'll consider it."

"Please do."

Cassian tugged open Belar's trousers.

There were no more words after that. They'd been stolen away by the feel of Cassian's hands on him. He was stretched between whatever Cassian's mouth was doing to his neck and the fingers curled around his prick. He moaned. Strained as he begged for more, faster, and it was given to him. He raked Cassian's side with one hand, fingers snagging on his shirt as the vampire's hiss of surprise brushed his ear, and then he was shoved forward, arms braced on the table as Cassian pushed him down and kept him there, the other stroking him hard. He was so completely covered. Contained. Held. That was all it took. He came with a cry that tore at his throat, so sharp he couldn't breathe, everything disappearing in one bright moment that shattered like stars.

*

Belar lay gasping and boneless on the table after as his breathing slowed and returned to normal. As the dazzle of stars fell out of his eyes. Feeling the tightness of Cassian's arms wrapped around him. They were the only thing keeping him from dropping onto the floor. Cassian brushed the hair from the back of Belar's neck, hesitating a moment before he laid a kiss there. He let a long tendril run through his fingers like ribbon.

"Is this going to happen every time I fuck you?" he asked in a soft voice.

Belar lifted his head and blinked bleary eyes at him. His mouth was dry, his hands stiff from clenching them into fists. And his hair had faded back to its true color again. Blue-gray strands curled around Cassian's fingers.

His glamour had broken along with the rest of him.

Belar shot upright, falling into Cassian's chest, stranded there by the hand in his hair and the jelly in his legs. "I—"

Cassian traced a finger along the faintly pointed tip of his ear, his real ear, and Belar leaned into the touch with a whimper despite himself. Oh stars, that felt good. Every touch buzzed against his hypersensitive skin until he could have melted again just from the right amount of pressure on his softest spots. He knew Cassian could find them. As though it were some kind of special instinct he possessed.

"It's not—" He had no idea how to finish the sentence. Or the one he had begun before. "Shit."

He sighed and turned to look up into Cassian's face.

He was smiling. "So, you have some Fae blood. My hunter does surprise," he purred. He tangled his fingers deeper into Belar's hair as he moved in for another slow, slow kiss that left Belar panting.

It wasn't the response he had expected.

"I'm yours now?" Belar lifted a brow as he wrapped both arms around his neck. "Are you sure?"

"I would like you to be." He nuzzled into the crook of Belar's neck again. "Unless you object."

It felt so easy to lean into his warmth. "Don't you have any questions about…?" Belar flapped one hand at his hair, his ears, his entire life thus far. "I expected there would be questions. And possibly some silent recriminations."

"No more than before, no." He laughed quietly, the huff of breath ruffling Belar's hair. "Darling, I'm a vampire. And now I live with Erathel and Arakiel. You'll have to work much harder than that to shock me. Did you *want* me to?"

Belar scowled. He really didn't know. This was completely uncharted territory for him. He reached up to brush the glamoured color back into his hair. The move was unnecessary, but it soothed him to do it. To reassure himself he looked as he wished. As always, he refused to interrogate that fear. "My father. He was Fae. Allegedly. It's a very long story and I've never spoken of it to anyone who didn't already know. I'm not sure I want to. At least not right now." He exhaled in one long gust until he felt empty again. Calm. Then he met Cassian's eyes. "I would much rather you took me upstairs and showed me what you look like without a shirt. I didn't get to enjoy it the first time."

"Oh really?"

"Maybe you could even do a little spin. Just so I don't miss anything."

One of Cassian's hands smoothed down his back as he leaned in for another kiss. "Is that all?"

"Give me time."

"That I can do."

Acknowledgements

Thank you all for your continued support of my deeply weird books and characters, for making a comfortable space, for allowing them to be different, and for giving me the courage to write yet another character with chronic pain.

And special thanks to my beta readers, sprinting partners, and everyone who listened to me ramble about how good Castlevania is (usually with gifs, many many gifs).

About the Author

J. Emery is slowly writing their way through every fantasy trope imaginable. And if they can make it weirder and queerer while they do, that's even better as far as they're concerned.

They spend their free time watching anime, gaming, and drinking large quantities of tea, occasionally all at the same time. They have also been known to document their ridiculous levels of terror while watching horror movies on twitter as @mixeduppainter. Sometimes they even discuss upcoming projects.

Email: mixeduppainter@gmail.com

Twitter: @mixeduppainter

Pinterest: www.pinterest.com/mixeduppainter

Also Available from NineStar Press

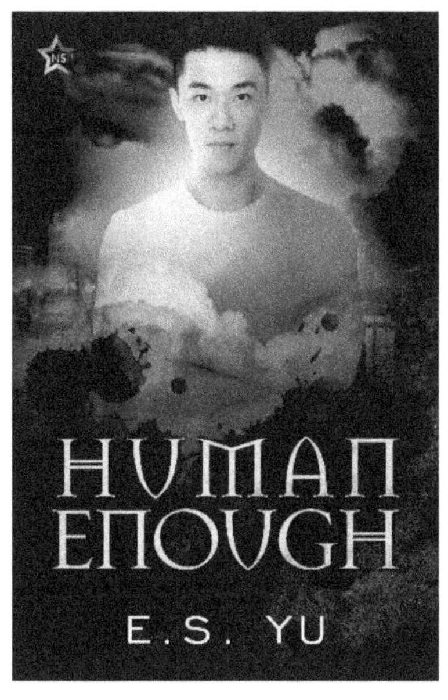

Connect with NineStar Press

www.ninestarpress.com

www.facebook.com/ninestarpress

www.facebook.com/groups/NineStarNiche

www.twitter.com/ninestarpress

www.tumblr.com/blog/ninestarpress

CPSIA information can be obtained
at www.ICGtesting.com
Printed in the USA
FSHW012013300320
68652FS